Praise f...

'Perfect for a single sitting on a winter evening, an easy, engrossing slip of a thing that explores the ultimate taboo' *Observer*

'Noli creates a tightly controlled thriller. Unease stirs from the opening paragraph . . . a tale of distressing plausibility' *Guardian*

'It's impossible not to be fascinated by this woman . . . You'll be compelled to keep reading to discover the truth' *She*

'Not only is the subject matter harrowing but the voice is cool and seductive, leading us inevitably to places we don't want to go; and yet, once there, unable to resist reading on. This psychological thriller is all the more terrifying because it touches on feelings common to more of us than we care to admit' *Age*

'A clever psychological thriller that puts inadmissible thoughts into well-chosen words' *Literary Review*

'Noli has woven a confronting and chilling tale'
Herald Sun

'A compellingly disturbing character . . . this book is hard to put down' *Sunday Telegraph*

'The watercooler book of the year' *Harper's Bazaar*

Camilla Noli lives in Australia with her husband and children. She is a graduate of the Varuna Writing Program in Sydney's Blue Mountains and the author of the critically acclaimed novel *The Mother's Tale*.

By Camilla Noli

The Mother's Tale
Broken Fences

BROKEN FENCES

Camilla Noli

An Orion paperback

First published in Great Britain in 2010
by Orion
This paperback edition published in 2011
by Orion Books Ltd,
Orion House, 5 Upper St Martin's Lane,
London WC2H 9EA

An Hachette UK company

1 3 5 7 9 10 8 6 4 2

A CIP catalogue record for this book
is available from the British Library.

ISBN 978-1-4091-2136-7

Printed and bound in Great Britain
by Clays Ltd, St Ives plc

The Orion Publishing Group's policy is to use papers
that are natural, renewable and recyclable products and
made from wood grown in sustainable forests. The logging
and manufacturing processes are expected to conform to
the environmental regulations of the country of origin.

www.orionbooks.co.uk

To my children, Luka and Tiana,
two of the wisest people I know

PROLOGUE

I am crying as I affix the tape to the window, the tears collecting on the end of my nose and then falling onto the carpet between my feet. I don't bother to wipe them away; I need both my hands to do this properly.

I work slowly, checking as I go that the seal is good, that not even the smallest space remains between the window and its frame. I am especially careful towards the bottom of the window where the end of the hose can just be seen protruding into the crack. I have closed the window as tightly as possible without compressing the rubber and I press the tape carefully here: several layers of it covering the window's opening and extending around the curved edges of the hose to hold it firm. Later, I will pull the curtain closed against the cold press of the outside world, and from within the room it will be impossible to see what I have done.

Tonight, when the children have finished their dinner and cleaned their teeth, when they have come into my bedroom with me and snuggled into bed against me, when the soft glow of the bedside lamp is the room's only illumination, when we have finished reading together, when the small amount of sleeping tablet I will have given them dissolved into warm chocolate has taken effect, then I will finish what I have begun. I will tiptoe to the garage and start the car. Ensuring the hose is still firm at that end, I will return to the bedroom and carefully push the rolled towel against the door; and then I will lie again between my children and wait, sealed inside this final chamber with the two people I love most in this world.

ONE

I watched them as they moved in that day, so long ago it seems, standing on my rear deck, looking over at the back of their house.

I watched as the other woman, my new neighbour, gave instructions to the removalists, sometimes hearing the cadence of her voice carrying for a moment above the cicadas' rhythmical singing. Her words did not carry, the house too far away, the voice modulated at too low a pitch, for that.

I watched her move through the rooms. The warm helmet of hair light in the sunshine, darker in the shadows. Perhaps she saw me and raised a hand at one time, initiating contact. I turned away as the movement was witnessed, so could not be sure.

The people in the house before had been elderly, used to their own company, not needing contact, intimacy. New neighbours would mean readjustments, realignments, the need for efforts which previously had not been expected. I knew that, but it was too early then to decide how I really felt about it. For that moment I had been happy to watch, and assess.

I could see that my new neighbour was used to giving instructions. Had thought about where each piece of furniture was to be placed; pointing and directing so that everything was where it should be in the first instance – nothing would be double-moved. An efficient woman. I had visited my previous neighbours, of course, so knew the layout of the house – not so different from my own: formal rooms to the front, bedrooms and a large rumpus at the back leading out to a deck with steps down to the heavily shaded back garden.

I watched as the removalists struggled up the back steps, taking those objects that were too large to carry through the house: an ornate, wooden queen-size bed, obviously for the master bedroom; a smaller double ensemble bed, probably intended for the spare room; office furniture; and then, a single, white, wrought-iron bed, the sort for which my daughter had been begging for months, with matching white bedroom furniture. So they had a daughter.

It was then that I saw the girl run around the side of the house, bounce up the back steps and come to a stop beside her mother. Blonde hair, blinding in the sun. *Her* words – demanding, strident – did carry; the voice of a child used to getting what she wanted. *There's no swing, Mummy. Daddy promised me there'd be a swing, like at our old house.* I could almost see her protruding bottom lip.

I didn't hear the mother's reply, but could imagine it. *Don't worry, Daddy will build you one just like he promised.* The voice low and soothing; the mother's hand lifted to the child's face. Life was easy for this girl, that was obvious, even at that early point. A child used to getting what she wanted; a mother willing to give it to her. An only child – the story was written in my head before I even knew the names of those I observed – loved, spoiled, angry. Perhaps not even a very nice girl at all.

I was in the kitchen at the sink when my daughter came running in shouting. 'Mummmmeeee, there's a girl over there!'

'There's no need to yell,' I said, turning slightly, the merest incline of a shoulder to indicate interest. 'And yes, I already know that.'

Beccy was dancing around behind me. 'Can we go over and say hello.' It wasn't a question. 'You know Mummy, there's a hole in the fence there as well. We can visit her the same way we visit Sammy and Tabby.'

I turned around then. 'You can, but you may not. Not now anyway. They're too busy. Her mummy's organising the house. We'll go over the day after tomorrow – the proper way – and say hello. We'll take something, a cake or flowers, and we'll all welcome them, together, properly. That will be the best way to do it.'

'Oh pleeeeease, Mummy, pleeeeease.' Beccy grabbed my hand, pulling backwards. 'She looks so nice. Why can't we go across and say hello now?'

I leaned down to her, removing some of the pressure of the insistent pull of her body, small yet almost unbearably heavy when she wanted it to be. 'No, Beccy. I've explained why you can't go and that's the end of the matter. We'll go together, tomorrow.' Already I'd conceded a day and both I and my clever daughter knew it. 'That's that. No arguing. Okay?'

Looking down at the ground, Beccy nodded and I thought that would be the end of it.

I was washing my hands in the bathroom when I happened to look out the window and see them, pushing their way through the rotten palings that made up the back fence. It was the damp that did it. Our former neighbours had told me many years before that there had once been a small creek flowing along the existing fence line, but that it had been drained and piped underground by the council. It always seemed romantic to me, to own land through which a creek had once flowed; I liked to imagine the children playing near that ancient, buried, watercourse.

Seeing my children that day, heading into unknown territory, I hesitated. If I called out to them there was a good chance they would ignore me; possibly the new neighbour would hear me and think I was unable to control my own children. So I let them go. Beccy looked back towards the house as she straightened up on the other side of the fence, and I knew then that she'd timed her sortie with precision, waiting until I was in the bathroom to slip over and taking Marty along with her, so that the potential punishment would at least be shared.

I shook my head; it was hard not to admire my daughter's determination even as I was frustrated by it. But it wasn't Beccy's fault entirely, I knew that. All children are like quicksilver, unable to be stopped, spreading themselves into corners their parents fear are too distant, dark, treacherous.

Later, the three children came out onto the deck, each of them with something in their hands. Watching from that distance it was hard for me to see what they were holding – muffins perhaps? They had been welcomed and fed, it seemed, and now they were making friends. There was already an easy intimacy in the way they moved: Beccy swinging from the rail at the top of the stairs; Marty settling on the middle step, peeling back the paper on his snack a bit at a time as he ate it, looking down to where the other girl stood, on the grass. Beccy began making big hand gestures and Marty nodded; the other girl laughed, her hair rippling. Suddenly, she ran down the stairs and began to hop up and down on one foot and then fell to the ground, playing the clown. Even from where I stood, I could see how irresistible she was: her fake clumsiness, the entertainment of it. Beccy finished her food and rushed down to join her, jumping in rhythm and falling, both of them always falling, together and apart, like two spineless jack-in-the-boxes. Once, the two girls fell together and bumped heads, but there was only laughter as they sat on the ground, each rubbing her own head and then that of the other.

And then, Marty had finished eating as well. He stood for a time near the girls at the bottom of the steps but didn't join their game, he sauntered instead deeper into the garden.

I saw the girls follow him, one blonde head and one brown flanking his taller frame, dancing, almost, around him.

The trio moved closer to the back fence, under the huge spreading tree that pressed a large part of the backyard into dappled shade and even threw its morning shadow over our fence. I could hear the children now. The blonde girl's voice rose clear into the morning air.

'Dad's going to build me a swing. Mum promised.' She pointed to the branches high above. 'He'll put it there. It'll be the longest swing ever and I'll swing really high, higher than the fence even. You can have turns on it. You can come over here any time you like. You'll both be my best friends.'

And then the three children were whispering to each other, heads already bowed together under the importance of whatever it is that kids say to each other when they believe their parents are well out of earshot.

When my children came home I questioned them about the new neighbours, not even bothering to reprimand Beccy for deliberately disobeying me.

'She told me she's a princess, Mummy, and her daddy is going to build her a swing. She said I can have goes on it. Marty too!'

I could see that my son was holding back, turning something over in his mind. 'What do you think, Marty?' I asked him, suddenly eager to uncover his view of this stranger with whom my daughter was already so enamoured.

'She's very . . .' He stopped, looking upwards and to the left as he always did when he was thinking. 'She's very . . . pretty.' And then he looked at me as if daring me to challenge him. It was the first time my son had noticed, or commented on, a girl's physical appearance. Nearly thirteen, he was tall and already slightly muscled, sometimes slow to use his mind, but never slow to use his body. And somehow it was that considered statement from my son that made me more wary about my new neighbours than any of my daughter's enthusiasms could have.

The next day I made my favourite chocolate cake, cooled it, iced it, and, with children in tow, made my way over to my new neighbours' house. Up the street, turning right at the intersection and then right again until the three of us stood in front of number 37, the block that abutted the back of ours. I made the children stand behind me while I knocked on the front door and introduced myself when it was opened. 'My name's Clair,' I said to the woman who opened it. Softly pretty in the late morning light, her hair was fair, but not nearly as blonde as her daughter's.

'I'm Sandy,' the woman responded. 'It's so lovely to meet you. Of course, your kids came over yesterday to see me and Chelsea. This is Chelsea.'

For the first time, I could examine the girl who stood beside her mother. Up close Chelsea was even prettier than I had imagined. Clear skin, blue eyes, clothes that were just right. I guessed that she was probably around eleven and, already, there was an effortless ease about her, a self-belief that had nothing to do with maturity. Even with that first glance I knew she was a girl I would find hard to like.

So in the end, I made contact with Sandy the proper way; was welcomed into her house, her lounge room, her life. I sat with her and talked while our children played together under our watchful gaze. This was how I wanted it to be; how I'd *imagined* it would be.

But it was too late, of course. The children had already made contact, they had already established the ground rules upon which the rest of our families' interactions would be based: the rules and the whims of children – informal, ad hoc, uncontrollable.

TWO

'Move over there, no there. Right. Stop. You three stay there.'

The children were playing outside that day. It is the last time I can remember the four of them – my kids and Sammy and Tabby from next door – playing alone like that, without Chelsea. There was an easy rhythm to their play, a spontaneity and a balance that those four children always had when they were together. It was because they had known each other for so long and so well; they'd virtually grown up together. So many of their games were variations on a theme, based on role-plays they'd been perfecting for years. There was an unselfconsciousness about their interactions – a real sense of fun and imagination

– that Marty and Beccy rarely displayed with other children, particularly as they became older.

That day they had thrown a blanket over a gap in the hedge to form a makeshift cubby and were planning what they were going to play. It was Marty speaking, doing his best to organise the others. 'Now I'm Sorcerer and my powers are that I can jump really high and I can disappear whenever I want to. All I have to do is turn around twice, and then twice again to reappear. And I can kill you by blinking at you, ummm . . . three times!'

It was Tabitha who spoke next. As usual she was dressed in a riot of colour, her shirt trailing behind her as she spun round and round. 'I'm Mirabelle and I can swim underwater without taking a breath, and everywhere that the garden is, is water.' Her arms swinging out wide to indicate the extent of her domain. 'So when I go there, in the garden, you have to swim and you can't catch me. And if I touch you with any part of my body I can drown you.'

Sam spoke after her. It was often like this, I'd noticed, the children taking turns in order of age. Sam concentrated hard as he considered his words. 'My power is that I have big scales for protection. That means no-one can kill me. And I can run really fast. And I have a stunning power, so I can kill people by holding out my hand. Kapow. Kapow. And I'm called, I'm called ANKLOSAUR.' His arms flung high and wide as he roared his name.

Beccy had been waiting while the others spoke, but not patiently. By the time it was her turn she was almost jumping up and down in her excitement.

'Well I have the *best* one; I can go back in time, so no-one can kill *me* because if anything happens to me I can change it.'

'Not if you're dead you can't.' Marty frowned at the absurdity.

'Yes I can.'

'No you can't. If you're dead you can't go back in time.'

'If you're dead you can do anything. And no-one can do anything to you.' She folded her arms. 'So I'll be completely safe.'

'That's ridiculous, Beccy! When you're dead you're dead, not safe! There's nothing after being dead, not even in a game. Otherwise what's the point of even playing?'

'That's right, Beccy.' Tabitha nodded. 'I'm sorry.'

'I'm not Beccy, I'm called, umm, I'm called TIME CHANGER.'

'So? You still can't go back in time if you're dead.'

'I'll do it just before I'm dead.'

'How? Nobody ever knows when they're going to die.'

'I just will.' Poor Beccy. I could hear the quiver in her voice; it sounded as if she was on the verge of tears.

'Well, I'm not going to play if you have that power. It's silly.' Marty turned to the other two. 'Sam and Tabby, do you agree?'

'Yeah! That's just silly.' Sammy, as was often the case, was not going to argue with Marty.

'Yeah, it is a bit unrealistic, Beccy.'

'So, Beccy, what other power do you have?'

'I'm . . . I'm . . .' Beccy's voice softened, collapsed. 'Ooooh, I want to be able to disappear tooooo. Marty, can I disappear like you?' Beccy put her hand on Marty's arm at that, imploring with her body as well as her voice.

'No! That's *my* power, you have to think of something else.' With a shrug of his shoulder Marty pushed aside her pleading hand.

'It's not fair. I'm always last and everyone else takes all the best powers.'

I knew that what Beccy was saying was true; she tried so desperately to keep up with the other, older, children, but so often it *was* a case of catch-up, Beccy tagging along behind as the others marched forwards. By this stage, her voice was definitely wobbly, her head lowered, shoulders hunched. I'd almost decided it was time to go downstairs and comfort her, tell the other kids – Marty in particular – to go a bit easier on her, when I saw Tabitha put her arms around Beccy, her shirt now trailing like butterfly wings down my daughter's back.

'I know,' said Tabitha brightly, 'why don't you be my sister in this game and we can *both* swim underwater?'

I saw Beccy's back relax, felt my own shoulders loosen. She looked up at Tabitha, smiling now. 'All right. Can I be the big sister?'

'Okay, you can be the big sister.' Tabby replied, giving Beccy a final little squeeze.

As the children disappeared beneath the blanket, I felt, yet again, the warm surge of relief, knowing that Tabitha and Sam were such good friends to my kids as well as being their neighbours. What wouldn't those four do for each other?

It was late afternoon by this time, and the hedge was one of the few parts of the garden still free from the shadow cast by the house. The leaves and the blanket were bathed in a golden glow as if painted on canvas. I imagined the children in their makeshift cubby, playing their make-believe games, within a warm cocoon of diffused light – sheltered, protected, safe.

That was what my life was like in those days. Carved, sculptured, managed. I thought I had been through a lot by then, and perhaps I had. I believed I'd reached a peaceful plateau, that there were no more slopes to negotiate. But such a state is only ever an illusion.

We all create our own lives and I'd done so more carefully than most. There are those who crave excitement, the lure of the unknown – the travellers, the adventurers – those who can throw in a job and not think too hard about where the next pay cheque will come from. And then there are those for whom safety is a need.

In those days I ensured there was an easy rhythm to my life. A warm suburban pulse. I worked two days each week at the local early childhood clinic steering mothers through the intricacies of those very early months and years: helping with feeding and sleep routines; giving vaccines and advice.

My days at home were spent doing all the jobs that mothers do – housework and cleaning, volunteer work for my children's schools. I balanced my life between these things, keeping myself busy enough to be able to remain content.

Sometimes, I would sit in the quiet of the lounge room, in those moments when we – the house and I – waited for the children to come home from school. It was as if we were breathing together in that sliver of peace – shallow, barely holding on. Even though I tried not to dwell on it too much, I knew that without the children, without the carefully regulated pace of my day, that house – my life – would be lonely, empty. Of course I had my husband, Peter, but even so I knew, had always known, that it was my children who breathed a soul into my existence, who filled my life with colour and substance. With them, within that carefully managed life, I had regarded myself and them as completely safe.

THREE

The next weekend I saw Chelsea's father for the first time. A compact man, stockier and stronger looking than my husband, but still with the air of a man who worked inside. He seemed slightly out of place in his own backyard, dressed in his 'weekend casual' clothes, surveying the sweep of his new territory. He had not been evident all week. Perhaps away, or simply working such long hours that he rose too early and came home too late to make an impact on the everyday life of his house.

It was the same with my own husband, and Mel's next door. The men working the long hours required to keep their families safe and happy in this leafy suburban neighbourhood, where people still called each other by name and it was safe to leave the door unlocked when you ducked down to the shop for a bottle of milk and a loaf of bread.

It was this man's wife who had done what I myself would have done for my husband and family, what so many women still do – borne the brunt of the load and orchestrated the move. There would have been just enough consultation throughout the process for him to feel that he wasn't entirely redundant, so that, one night, he would have found himself in his new home largely settled in, pleased with the contribution he had made.

That day, this man had obviously been given his job to do. I watched as he set up a work table in the backyard under the spreading tree, and ran out an electrical cord for the appliances he would use, still in their boxes, seemingly newly purchased especially for this task. The position of the work table, the way in which he moved, it was as if he was doing something he truly enjoyed. It could mean only one thing – he was building Chelsea's swing. So the girl had been right to be so sure of getting what she wanted.

The house was quiet that day. I was home alone. Saturday morning was generally Peter's time with the children. He took Marty to soccer, Beccy to dancing. He chatted with the other parents, took oranges that he'd cut up and chilled the night before (when he remembered), took his stint on the barbecue when he was on the roster, helped pull on ballet shoes and tidy hair buns that had worked themselves loose. All this was a form of relaxation for him, a game almost; the required tasks – so different from the stresses of his weekday job – were not taken seriously enough to cause him, or the children, any pressure. The children loved those mornings – dedicated, relaxed time – with their dad. Sometimes I went with them, but more often I stayed home, and that's why, that day, I was able to stand, quiet and still, at one of the back windows and watch.

I watched as my new neighbour took the pre-cut extra-long piece of wood that would form the seat of the swing. I watched as he planed and sanded it, then carefully marked and drilled the four holes through which he would thread the rope. He unpacked each tool as it was required, and repackaged it as he finished with it.

There can be no pretence in someone's behaviour when they are unaware they are being observed. I saw that man work without haste, calmly and methodically. In the care that he took over that small job and the obvious pleasure he gained from it, I could see just how much he loved his daughter. At times he would stop to admire what he had done – running his hand over the grain of the wood, feeling the smooth edge of his drill hole – as if he was creating a work of art and not merely a child's plaything.

When it was time to varnish the seat, he laid it on the work table, dipping his brush into the gloss, running it back and forward over the wood until it shone; the movement rhythmic, almost mesmerising. It was warm where I stood and I leaned against the window, relaxed and at peace, caught up in another's world, removed, for a time, from the realities of my own.

It was the creak of the garage door that jolted me from my reverie. The sound of Peter and the children coming home: bags thumped in the corridor; the beat of feet on the floor; the clatter of car keys dropped onto the table. Life returning to chaotic normality.

It was time to join my family, time to prepare lunch, time to stop my indulgent watching.

Saturday lunch has always been a simple affair in my house: cold meat, salad, sometimes roast left over from the night before. As usual, we sat in the kitchen together that day and the children told me about their morning. I remember Marty had scored a goal and won his game; Beccy was learning a new, complicated, dance routine. Such simple things, events so common they occupied only a small part of my mind. There are so many things we take for granted, every minute of every day. With the ebb and flow of that familiar conversation, I almost forgot about the man from the house behind us until Peter came back from the bathroom, flicking his thumb towards the garden.

'What's he doing over there?'

'Making a swing, I think.'

Beccy's head swung around. 'Oh, is he making a swing for Chelsea? She's going to be so excited!'

'Pretty expensive swing,' Peter commented. 'It looks like he's bought everything new – the drill, the plane, even the work table looks new. He'll probably hardly ever use any of it again. I could have lent him those things; he didn't have to buy all that new stuff.'

Peter sounded slightly wistful and I knew what he was thinking. When we were first married, he'd kitted himself out with the best of tools and had even had the time to use them. He'd made an outdoor table and the surrounds for the barbecue at the first house we'd owned; he'd even laid our first lot of pavers. That was a while ago, and now most of the tools were carefully stored, unused. Peter had no time and it was easier to pay someone to do the odd jobs around the house. But we both knew that in the other man's position, Peter would have done the same thing. There are certain jobs that a father should be able to do for his children. Just as there are certain things a mother must do.

'I wonder if he needs some help.' Peter was rubbing his hands together; he was itching to go over, but the job was almost too small to occupy one man sufficiently, let alone two.

'Maybe later,' I suggested. I'd watched the other man. I thought that he was happy to be working on his own.

Later, packing the dishwasher, I listened to my children talk as they sat in front of the television.

Beccy, as usual, couldn't remain still, bouncing up and down on the couch as she spoke. 'I hope,' – bounce, bounce – 'she invites us,' – bounce, bounce – 'to have a go.' Extra big bounce.

'I'm sure she will.' Marty was channel-surfing, flicking back and forward with the remote.

'I like Chelsea, she's fun.' Bounce, bounce. 'She's got the nicest room.' Bounce, bounce. 'I wonder where she is.' Bounce, bounce. 'Maybe she'll be round tomorrow and we can have a go on the swing.' By the end of her pronouncements, and her bouncing, Beccy was breathing hard.

'Yeah, that'd be good,' said Marty. I held my breath, curious about what he might add. But all I could hear was the continued switching of channels. Obviously that day's televised soccer game hadn't yet started.

'Let's go outside and see if Chelsea's home. Do you want to come outside, Marty?'

'She's not home, Beccy, or else she'd be with her dad, I'm sure.' Marty sounded faintly irritated, although whether it was with Beccy or the television, I couldn't tell. 'I reckon her mum's taken her out somewhere while her dad makes the swing for her as a surprise.'

'Ooooh, she's going to be soooo happy when she gets home.' Another big bounce. 'I can't wait to have a go.'

I went back to watching again. I couldn't help myself. It was as if I'd seen the first act of a play and had to know how it ended. By now my new neighbour had hung two heavy ropes for the swing from a very high branch and was threading them through the holes he'd drilled in the seat. The ropes were specially tied with some kind of complicated knot so they wouldn't slip. It was all carefully done, this one job in the family's move for which Chelsea's father had been given sole responsibility.

Finally, when all was finished, he sat, for a moment, on the swing's seat – so wide and deep that it could easily accommodate even him – pushing gently up and down with his toes, his legs slightly too long for it to be really comfortable. Yet he looked, content, and I remembered what I'd read during my early nursing training, about the power of movement – swinging in particular; how humans gain pleasure and reassurance from a gentle rocking backwards and forwards. It's how even the most restless baby can be calmed, and I recalled that I'd used this technique with my own children, many times.

That swing had the power to soothe and bring comfort. It looked sturdy and strong and I had watched almost every step of its construction. I had seen that Chelsea's father was a thorough man and had built the swing with care, but – now that the swing's true scale was apparent – I could also see that he had made a swing that would know no bounds. It was a swing that would not be controlled once it had begun; a swing so generous that it would allow Chelsea, and whoever she invited to use it, to swing as high as the top of the fence – and perhaps even higher. And because it was a swing which had been built for a child's use and pleasure, not for the man who now sat on it, adults would have absolutely no control over the way it would be used. Here, I saw, was danger, pressed firmly against our broken back fence.

My previous calm had fled and, agitated now, I began to turn away from the window just as Peter, wanting to have his own look, came up behind me, placing his arms either side of me, trapping me against the glass.

Peering over my shoulder, Peter spoke: 'Oh good, he's finished.' Releasing me, he moved into the kitchen; I heard the sound of the fridge opening and closing before he bounded down the back stairs across to the fence and called to the other man, holding out a beer, condensation already forming on the bottle in the afternoon heat.

They leaned over the fence together, the two men, laughing as if they had known each other for a lifetime. At least *they* were too big to crawl under the fence like the children, I thought as I looked at them; at least *they* were contained by decorum and social niceties, by the fences that were supposed to delineate spaces of individual responsibility and obligation, by the fences that were meant to act as a barrier and not be ignored.

As I stood watching them for a little longer, I wondered about Sandy and Chelsea. What were they doing to fill the time while the swing was being built: were they out shopping, buying new clothes or more knick-knacks for Chelsea's room? I pictured the movement of mother and daughter, fair head and fairer head pressed close together.

I looked at the clock then and realised it was time for me to head out shopping myself. So I knew that I wouldn't see the end of this particular act: Chelsea's squeal of delight when she saw the swing; the pleasure on the faces of her parents; her first go on the wonderful new toy. But I had been able to imagine it, the small family drama that would be played out in the perfect afternoon sunlight. Just one of many performances that make up all our lives.

FOUR

When I leaned over the fence all those months ago, when everything was still forming, when events could have gone many ways, I was mimicking the actions of my husband the weekend before, except this time it was the fence to the right side of our house that I was leaning against, and it was my long-time neighbour, Mel, to whom I was talking. Mel, the mother of Tabitha and Sammy, my children's closest friends, friends who were as warm and predictable as a blanket.

'Have you met the new people who've moved in behind us?' Mel asked me. She had just finished hanging out the washing and I could see the movement of the sheets on her clothes line. She did her bed sheets on Thursdays. We regularly spoke at this time; it was never arranged, we simply often found ourselves outside at the same time.

'Yes,' I nodded. 'I went over the day after they arrived, but the kids had already visited, through the hole in the back fence.'

Mel laughed at that, her face relaxed in the sunlight. 'Sometimes I don't know why we bother with fences at all. It's not like our kids pay any attention to them.'

'Yes, but our kids are such good friends, they've known each other for so long that it's okay.'

'And I guess it's more fun than having a gate. That'd make their visits completely legit and who'd want that!' She laughed again, her head thrown back; I could see the blue-green vein in her neck.

'That's the whole trick, isn't it?' I replied. 'Let them feel adventurous when really they're completely safe. It's the whole trick of mothering really.'

Mel touched me on the arm. 'Darl, you analyse these things far too much.'

Casually I moved my arm from beneath her hand, shifting my body so that I was looking towards our new neighbours' house, bright in the mid-morning sun. 'They have a daughter, Chelsea,' I told Mel. 'She's very pretty. Marty's quite taken by her and Beccy's adopted her as her new best friend and older sister.'

Mel tucked her hands under her arms and looked towards the house as well. 'We'll have to introduce ourselves soon. How old is she, do you know? Would she be about the same age as Tabitha?'

'Yeah, probably.'

'Good. It'll be nice for Tab to have another girl around the same age as her. I mean, I know she and Beccy are like sisters, but, you know, it'll be great for Tabby to have a "grown-up" friend almost next door.'

I nodded, but felt the lurch of my heart, for suddenly I did know. Beccy's new best friend would not remain within her exclusive possession forever. As a parent you are never ready to contemplate your child's first rejection.

Oblivious to the effect of her words, Mel continued. 'And it's funny you should say that Marty's already keen on her. Sammy was just saying the other day how there's a new girl in his class who's very pretty, and he's only ten!' Mel fixed me with her warm brown eyes. 'They're growing up. Looking at girls, noticing what they look like. We can't stop it; we shouldn't *want* to stop it. Before we even know it, they'll be bringing their girlfriends home to meet us.' She shook her head, smiling. 'Like they say, it all happens in the blink of an eye.'

I didn't smile; instead I regarded the house behind us. It seemd to have a fresh energy circulating round it since the new neighbours had moved in. The recently erected swing was moving back and forward slightly in the wind.

'What's the mother like?' Mel asked. 'What's her name anyway?'

'Sandy,' I replied and then shrugged. 'She's like us, I guess. From what I can tell, her husband works long hours. He put up the swing on the weekend, but that's the only time I've seen him. I don't know whether she works part-time or not, but I don't think so.'

'I think I'll go over tomorrow and introduce myself, take a bunch of flowers, do it while the kids are at school. See what I think of her as well.' Mel looked directly at me again. 'You know, in a way, I wish my kids had gone over and introduced themselves like yours did. I mean, let's face it, the sooner the kids feel comfortable going over the better. Take a bit of pressure off us, spread the load.'

'Marty and Beccy already feel comfortable going over there,' I replied with a bit of a laugh, wondering, even then, why it was a statement that made me so uneasy.

FIVE

I was cleaning up in the lounge room when, from the direction of the backyard, an unfamiliar voice, shrill enough for me to hear even at the front of the house, began to call. 'Hell-o, hell-o, hell-o!'

I moved to the laundry window to see what was happening. It was Chelsea, her head poking over the fence, her hands curled around her mouth to form a makeshift megaphone, calling to my children who, with Tabitha and Sam, were playing around the side of the house. There was no hint of hesitation in Chelsea's voice; she was a confident child, sure of her welcome. 'What're you playing?' she yelled.

The other children made their way over to the fence where Chelsea stood, Beccy so short she had to jump to show her face above the palings, desperate not to miss out on anything. Her fine brown hair rising and falling as she leaped.

At that distance I couldn't hear what was said, even though I quietly slid the window open as far as I could, but soon I saw Chelsea's head duck down and her body appear on the same side of the fence as the others, disappearing around the side of the house with the rest of the children.

It was inevitable, I knew, that this would occur – Chelsea joining with my children and Mel's. I'd been waiting for it to happen, the moment when she'd push her way through the fence and into our lives: confident, impatient, demanding. But there was little I could do about it, I knew that also. Sometimes spaces have to be created, even for what is not directly welcomed. And so I turned back to my house that day, ready to prepare dinner, unpack backpacks, sort out school notes for the next day – concerned only with the everyday minutiae that erodes so much of our lives.

It was only when I went into my bedroom at the back corner of the house, to hang up my jacket, that I heard it – Chelsea's voice, raised and strident. 'That's a silly game,' she was saying, her voice ugly with derision. 'I don't want to play that game anymore. I want to play a different game.'

I looked out the window and saw the children moving around the backyard, like birds that have been scared from their perch, ducking and wheeling, searching for a safe place to alight once more. I knew they were willing to oblige the newcomer: easygoing, non-confrontational, they would be happy to play anything at all, but I also knew that Chelsea – with both her presence and her words – had upset the previous easy balance of the game and that now a new fulcrum was being established.

Even as I watched, the game shifted and rearranged itself. Soon there were two groups: the boys and the girls. And then, suddenly, there were three: the boys; Chelsea and Tabitha; and my daughter – Beccy – off to one side by herself, completely alone, isolated, vulnerable. And then she was moving towards the house, crying.

Pushing open the back door and letting it slam behind her, she found me partway down the corridor. I had already begun to move towards her, and we met in the darkest part of the hall. 'They won't let me play,

Mummy.' Even in that dim light I could see that her eyes were wet and shiny. 'They keep giving orders and telling me what to do and they said that I'm too small and silly to play the game they're playing. Tabby called me a baby.' Beccy hung her head, let her body fall into mine, and that was when it happened.

In that moment – a sliver of time when I was vulnerable and exposed, concerned for my daughter and angry about what had been done to her – I felt it all return, those feelings I hadn't experienced for years, had hoped never to have to let into my life again. The ropy weight of old rejection rose from the hidden recesses of my gut to rest firmly against the front of my throat – constricting, damaging, causing a film to cover my eyes and the pulse of my heart to pound within my ears. A reaction so physical, so overwhelming, that for a moment it was as if I was back in my own childhood and couldn't breathe, could find no way of escape. It was a reaction which, if purely personal, would have been enough to make me seek the warm safety of bed. It was in that short, short period of time that I discovered there truly *are* things you learn from your children: and what I learned was that old hurts and rejections are not forgotten, that they lie dormant, waiting for the time to be right to resurface and let you know they have not gone, that you are not free, that you will never be free of them.

But, of course, this reaction was not purely personal, it was not for myself, it was for my daughter, my beloved Beccy, who had been excluded – in her own backyard! It was as if every one of my emotions had been crystallised and sharpened, turning and tumbling within my body, cutting and embedding themselves. And I knew exactly who was to blame. Tabby had never spoken before in such a way to Beccy. It was that girl, that Chelsea, who had caused Beccy to be bullied in a place where she should have been supremely safe.

This was a talent some people possessed, I knew that. Even though it could be developed, it could not be learned; it was simply what some people *had* – the power to turn others with a word, a phrase, a look, a gesture. There were those with the ability to inject a poison and then stand back and watch others suffer for what came from it; I had experienced this before and done nothing about it then. But this time, in this space, there was something I could do.

'Into your bedroom, Beccy,' I instructed.

'But Mummy . . .'

'INTO. YOUR. BEDROOM.'

As my daughter moved, so did I. I did not prevent the back door from banging as I usually would have. I took the stairs two at a time. I stood in front of the children with my hands on my hips, imagining the fire in my eyes, the children quailing before me. As they looked up at me, the blue light of Chelsea's gaze professed an innocence that, like smothering water, would have drenched a lesser fire. But I was not to be stopped.

'It's time for you kids to go.' I waved my hands in the direction of Chelsea and Tabitha, sweeping over just enough to include Sam in the dismissal. I still had control, here. 'Martin, it's time for you to go inside and have some quiet time.'

'But Mum . . .'

'INSIDE. NOW. Tabitha, Sammy, Chelsea, thank you for coming, but now it's time to go home. You can come back when you can play together nicely.'

The look out of lowered lids . . . I knew that Chelsea was aware of exactly why she and the others were being sent home.

Half an hour later, happy screams caused me to look, again, out the window. Chelsea, Tabitha and

Sammy were running happily around Mel's back garden. Their yelling was perfectly modulated: not loud enough to be shushed by Mel, but sufficiently piercing to carry to where two closed doors and a television turned up high were not quite enough to stop their squeals and laughter from reaching the ears of my unhappy children.

It was the first time they all played together, those five children, but I knew it would be far from the last.

SIX

I had been invited to sit at Sandy's kitchen table, less proper than the formal combined dining and lounge room where I'd been entertained the first time I'd come over, chocolate cake in hand, children in tow. The space in which we sat that day was more suitable for entertaining someone who was regarded already, simply, as a friend. I could see that Sandy had renovated the kitchen. I couldn't be sure exactly when it was done, but it must have been prior to them moving in; there wouldn't have been time since. The previous heavy timber doors and benchtops had been replaced with shiny white doors, stainless steel handles and black granite benchtops which glittered when the overhead lights were turned on.

Sandy giggled like a little girl opening a much coveted present when she turned on those lights. 'It's something I really wanted, these sparkling benchtops. I saw them once, in a display house, and swore that one day I'd design and build a home around them. It was the compromise when we moved here, to a house that was already built. I said that I'd come, so long as I was allowed to put in my glittering benchtops. And *voilà*! Here they are.'

Sandy looked at me seriously then. 'Clair, I'm so happy David talked me into looking in this area. It's so much nicer than some of those soulless new estates we were originally thinking of building in. And I wouldn't have met you, of course, and Chelsea wouldn't have had so many wonderful friends to play with.'

'It's nice for me to have you here as well,' I replied carefully. 'The Robertsons were good neighbours ... well, quiet anyway, but we never really had anything in common. If the kids kicked a ball over the fence, it was always such a bother to collect it.'

Sandy smiled. 'There's no need to worry about that now. Marty and Beccy are welcome here any time. My home is your home, that type of thing.' She stopped moving around the kitchen, sat down and lightly touched my arm, warm and engaging. 'The truth is, Clair, that I'm so happy to have some friends here, people who'll just drop in. David works such long hours and with Chelsea getting bigger and more independent every day I used to get lonely in our old house. I'm hoping that we'll become friends, true friends.'

It was what I wanted too, of course, I knew that. Friends are the cement of a community, they are there for you when you need them, they are insurance, they help keep your children safe. I was not about to reject her offer of friendship, either for myself or my children. Even then, I could see that there was a depth to Sandy, shades of dark and light, of understanding and strength, a balance in her make-up that was not only attractive, but for me – who had always sought such harmony – almost irresistible.

I was shown around the house that day. Chelsea's room was completely pink and white, filled with every conceivable luxury a girl of her age could desire: the fully stocked dressing-table; the white computer on its specially designed desk; the cupboard filled with the latest clothes. Sandy showed it all to me, proudly. 'It's my failing. I can't deny her anything, but then she's my only child. I was bleeding so badly after she was born that I had to have a hysterectomy. I'll never have any more children, Clair; Chelsea will never have a brother or sister. I hope she'll be close to your children. I don't think you know how much I hope for that. I see how your kids play with Tabitha and Sammy. They're close to each other, so good for each other. I hope Chelsea can fit into that as well.'

I hoped for that too, of course – believe me, it's what I would have liked most of all.

Chelsea was on the swing, pushing herself higher and higher, shrieking with pleasure, and like a child watching the most magnificent of magical tricks, Beccy was caught, standing on the back deck, a mixture of delight and envy on her face. Somehow Chelsea saw her there and called out to her. 'Come over, come over and have a swiiiiiinnnng.' The last word dying away as Chelsea swooped towards the ground.

In a moment Beccy was beside me, begging as only she could. 'Can I go Mummy, please, can I please go over and have a swing?' Under normal circumstances Beccy might not have asked for my permission, but I'd made it clear to my children how dangerous I thought that swing looked. That way I had hoped they would at least be careful.

I considered for a time while Beccy continued to plead. 'Please Mummy, please.' And then I relented. 'All right darling, but you're not to go as high as Chelsea's going now. Do you promise me that you'll swing lower than that?'

Beccy nodded enthusiastically. 'I promise, Mummy, I really do. I promise. I promise. Thank you!' Running outside, she called to Chelsea. 'I'm coming!' And within a moment she had slipped under the back fence.

I watched the two girls – quite deliberately; I wanted them to *see* me watching. Beccy waved to me a few times and I waved back. 'Stay and watch me Mummy,' she called out. And I would have stayed until she finished playing, but then I heard the phone ring.

'Back in a sec,' I called out to Beccy, waving to her once more as I pushed open the back door. She was all right, I could see that. Chelsea was being careful. Beccy had always insisted that she didn't know how to swing herself – even though Peter and I had regarded that assertion with deep suspicion for some years – and Chelsea was standing behind her, gently pushing the seat.

It was Rose on the phone, the treasurer of Marty's school's Parents and Friends Committee. I'd taken over the role of president at the beginning of the year when the committee had appeared to be in danger of folding. It was only Marty's first year at the school and the position was demanding, but I enjoyed it. The team I'd pulled together was a mixture of my friends and parents of Marty's friends, so we knew each other and worked together well. Most importantly we were all enthusiastic. Rose and I had a number of financial issues to discuss that day, which took some time. So it was only when I put the phone down that I heard it, Beccy screaming. 'Stop Chelsea, stop! You're pushing me too high!'

Running outside, right down to the fence, I saw Chelsea pushing with the whole force of her body, almost doubled over after the effort of the thrust. I saw Beccy's white knuckles taut around the ropes, legs straight and stiff with fear, the rigid cast of her back. She was looking towards our house, watching desperately for me to come and save her.

'Stop!' I screamed. There was no subtlety in my tone – 'Stop, you stupid girl!' – or language.

Chelsea responded by halting the swing quickly, too quickly, so quickly that it was dangerous. The swing spun around, Beccy's small body jerking as the seat came to rest. As soon as it fully stopped she jumped off, unsteady on the ground, her face tight, her breath coming in short puffs.

I extended my arms over the palings, stretching out to my daughter, so close to me but unreachable, the barrier of the fence immovable as she stood alone in her fear.

Turning my face to Chelsea, I twisted my mouth, trying hard not to swear at her, not to utter the words of vitriol that were inside my head. 'What were you thinking?' is what came out instead. 'Why were you pushing her so high?'

'She was enjoying it; it was a game.'

'A game? A game! Look at her! She's petrified.'

'But she told me to push her higher. She kept saying, "Higher and higher". Didn't you, Beccy? Tell her!'

Beccy hung her head.

'Tell her, Beccy. Did you want to be pushed higher or not?'

Beccy nodded.

'But not that high,' I responded. 'Surely you knew that, Chelsea. She's a lot younger than you. You should have had more sense.'

'I was just doing what she wanted.'

'That's ridiculous, Chelsea, she would never have wanted you to push her like that.' Looking towards my daughter I calmed my voice. 'Are you all right, Beccy? Come here, darling. Come over here.'

'But Mummy, I'm not ready to come home yet.'

'Come here now, Beccy.'

Moving towards me, Beccy ducked under the fence, over to my side. I leaned down to her, wrapped my arms around her. 'Are you all right darling? Are you all right?'

She nodded. Without a backward glance at Chelsea, I brought Beccy inside, with me, to a place where at that time I truly believed her to be safe.

SEVEN

We were spending the weekend away together, as a family. It was something we did as often as we could afford to. Usually we went away between school terms, when the children's sports didn't occupy the weekend, but that week Marty had a bye and we'd decided Beccy could miss one week of dancing. Unexpectedly, we'd run into one of my work colleagues also away with her family. The children were almost the same age and they'd body-boarded and swum together in the surf all day. As a result, the kids were already in bed, sleeping the sleep of the exhausted. I'd been in the surf that day as well and my head felt heavy, waterlogged. I felt sure that, full of surf and sun and sand, relaxed and at ease, I would sleep deep and long.

Peter and I were in bed reading, books propped against our knees, bedside lights on, breathing in synch. My eyes were almost closing and I'd decided that it was nearly time to turn off the light when Peter jammed his book down on the bedside table, and spoke. 'Dave seems like a good bloke.'

'Who?' I asked. I wasn't in the mood for conversation with its potential to drag me from the edges of sleep.

'Dave, the bloke who's moved in behind us.'

The men had been together again the weekend before, leaning over the fence, sharing a beer. That time there had been no swing to bind them, but somehow it had happened: the two of them finding themselves outside at the same time. One of them pulled some beers from the fridge and they'd stayed talking until night fell and – like the children they'd once been – they were called inside for dinner, this time by wives rather than mothers. Unlike their children, the men would never duck under the fence; unlike us women they would probably never build their friendship around shared conversations within each other's houses, or that would come only if the women organised it for them. No, instead there'd be the impromptu beer while hanging over the comfortable support and separation of the fence and then, maybe later, a game of tennis or golf or a trip to the football. I knew this pattern. It wasn't a threat.

'Oh yes, Sandy's husband.' I turned the page, interested enough to respond but not so interested that I'd stop reading. I wanted to finish my chapter before sinking into sleep.

'I was thinking about how much the kids enjoyed themselves today . . . you know, having some other kids their own age to play with, and I was thinking maybe we could do something with both our families, Dave's and ours. You know, go camping or something.'

I rested my book on the covers. 'Camping? When have we ever gone camping?'

'Well, I've been thinking about it for a while, you know that. It'd be cheaper than staying somewhere like this. Maybe if we camped we could go away more often. Dave says they've got a lot of gear. We won't have to rough it too much.' Peter laughed and reached over to pick up my hand. 'I know how you like your hot showers. We'd go somewhere civilised;

somewhere peaceful where we can relax and put our feet up and the kids can have some time together. We could invite Mel and Joe's mob as well.'

He began to stroke the top of my hand. 'It'd be nice, Clair. I used to love camping as a kid, and we've never taken Marty and Beccy. They'd love it.'

'But Peter, it doesn't make sense. We see our neighbours all the time, almost every day.'

'You might, but I don't, and anyway the kids get on so well. It'll be an adventure for them to go away together.'

'But we have weekends like this, away, so we can spend time together as a family, not with other people. It can be a bit intense, you know, being together with neighbours all the time, that's all.'

Peter turned to look at me. 'Don't you like her? What did you say his wife's name was? Sandy?'

I shook my head. Peter and I had known each other since our early days of university. He knew so much about me, but this had always been hard for me to explain to him. I liked and needed people, enjoyed their company, but at the same time things had happened to me that made it difficult for me to completely trust other people enough to let them too deep into my life. I always felt as if I needed to hold something back, keep something in reserve. And then, of course, there was my distrust of Chelsea.

'I like Sandy, I do, but we have to be a bit careful. You're not home all the time like I am, like the kids are. I think it'd be a mistake to take a holiday together, that's all. I mean on top of all the time we spend together anyway.'

Peter turned fully onto his side and began to stroke my forehead. 'We don't have to do anything you don't want to. You know that, don't you? Think about it. It's just that I think we'd all really enjoy doing something together like that.'

I lay awake for a long time that night running Peter's words through my head. I wished some things were as easy for me as they appeared to be for him.

You see, I believed then that there was a balance in life, a delicate balance that could be achieved. We already mixed with Sandy and Mel and their families without effort – how much better then to spend our spare holiday time either alone as a family or with other people, people who could expand our children's circle of friends, and ours? I often wondered what it would be like to not have to worry constantly about these things, to be able to contemplate camping trips with neighbours as easily as Peter obviously did.

That night I still believed that every action has a consequence which is set firmly in stone, which then in turn will influence everything that comes after it. I believed in the importance of treading carefully in life . . . so very, very carefully, with everything marked, everything measured, everything controlled; that night I still believed that such care, such vigilance, was necessary, that it was enough.

EIGHT

I'd barely begun to warm up when I heard
her calling. 'Clair, Clair, do you have a
moment?' She was standing on her front steps and I
wondered if she'd been waiting for me, if she knew
and followed my routine well enough for that.

I stopped walking and took out my earplugs, but
waited, by the letterbox, for her to continue.

Sandy inclined her head towards her house. 'Do
you have time to come in?'

I hesitated, not wanting to fully break my morning
schedule, but not knowing how I could refuse. Sandy
knew as well as I did that what was waiting for me
at home was merely the housework. I had largely
devoted my life to my family and, as my children

grew older and more independent, the rhythm of my week was hardly frantic, even with my part-time and volunteer work. And yet, I *did* have a rhythm, a routine. I'd learned that there is a pacing to all stages of parenthood. In the early days, at home with a baby, there are great swathes of time when you feel incredibly busy – and yet nothing much happens. Day follows day almost interminably, tied to the rhythms of sleeping, playing and eating, largely determined by the whims of your child. I remember once reading a book called *An Endless Afternoon*, a selection of writings about parenthood. That's exactly what it can feel like with children sometimes, like an afternoon that stretches into nothingness, nothing significant achieved or done, just another indeterminate period of time to add to a string of others. And as you are filling this time, shrinking and aging, your children grow and blossom, increasingly independent, moving further away from you with each passing day. I've coped with this by establishing my own routines, marking out my days with the daily habits that keep my mind and body busy, occupied.

But there was to be no refusal of Sandy that day; my politeness was so ingrained that the need for a walk, to maintain the routine of that particular day, was nowhere near strong enough to plane it away.

And so I followed Sandy inside. The house was immaculate at – I glanced at my watch – 8.45. My kids had just been put on the bus and I hadn't even cleaned up the breakfast dishes. I tried to put that from my mind as I sat with Sandy at her table, wondering exactly what it was this woman did to fill *her* days.

Without even offering me the customary cup of tea or coffee, Sandy began. 'Look, I might as well just plunge right in. The thing is that Chelsea hasn't settled into her new school very well. I made a mistake in the selection. I really should have done more research.'

I nodded. 'I know how hard it is. It's really important to get your children into the school that's right for them.' It was something I'd agonised over with both my children, particularly with high school. In fact I'd often told Peter that if we moved again before the children left school, it would have to be within the same school district.

I heard the gentle puff of Sandy's exhaled breath, saw the drop of her shoulders. 'Oh, I'm so glad you understand, Clair. And of course now that I've looked into things, all the best schools have waiting lists as long as my arm, and I just hate to see Chelsea as miserable as she is.'

I nodded again, but a miserable Chelsea was hard for me to imagine; she was a girl who seemed to know exactly what she wanted and how to get it.

Sandy shrugged. 'There's not a lot I can do about it now. It's the last year of primary and she'll just have to make do for the rest of this year. But I really wanted to talk to you about high school, Clair. I've done all my research, and as far as I can tell it's the school that Marty's going to that I'd really like to get Chelsea into. It's got such a great performing arts focus and that's the type of thing Chelsea absolutely loves.' She paused. 'The problem is they've put her on a waiting list and there are over seventy kids in front of her. They told me that her chances of getting in next year are very slim.'

'I'm sorry to hear that,' I replied carefully, my voice measured. I'd begun to understand why Sandy had called me in.

'Anyway, Clair, I was hoping you'd be able to help me. I was thinking that if you'd be prepared to write me a reference they'd look more kindly on my application. They've already hinted as much. When

I mentioned that I knew you, they told me at my interview what a great president of the Parents and Friends you are, and how you've already made great contributions to the school even though Marty's only been there a short time.'

Sandy stopped and I considered what she'd told me. The fact was that I knew the school *should* be grateful for my efforts. As well as taking on the role of president of the P & F I'd even got a few new committees set up: the education committee, the welcoming committee, the care group. I enjoyed my participation, but it did help, of course, that being president benefited Marty at the school. When I needed something done, the teachers listened and I knew that Marty was always looked out for.

But Sandy was asking me to use my influence for Chelsea, with the result that if I was successful she would be attending school with Marty next year, and with Beccy in a few years' time.

I liked Sandy, but getting her child into the same high school as Marty was another thing altogether. Chelsea and Marty already spent so much time together and she wasn't a child I particularly liked anyway. And what of the presence of Sandy herself? I wondered about that as well. How would Sandy being at Marty's school affect my standing with the other parents, the other mothers? I didn't know Sandy well enough to be sure. Would she prove to be friend or foe, support or hindrance? With her easygoing manner, her warmth, her wit, there was even the possibility that she would become better friends with the women at Marty's school than I was myself. I felt my heart pounding, a haze settling before my eyes; Sandy's request was something I didn't want to have to make a decision on. When they already spent so much time together at home, I was glad that their different schools acted as a barrier of sorts between our children, between our families; what I didn't know was whether that was something I was prepared to breach.

Even as I considered those things, even as my mind raced with indecision, my body betrayed me – my hand reaching out to the other woman, placing itself on the soft flesh of the top of her arm. 'Of course, Sandy,' I replied. 'Of course I'll try to get Chelsea into Marty's school.'

Sandy leaned over and hugged me then, her cheek soft against mine, her hand fluttering against my back, her words thankful in my ear.

I'd known, of course, that really there'd been no choice in my response. It was my weakness, the inability to say no to something when asked. So how could I have done anything other than what Sandy asked me to do? There was no way I could have laid out my shameful reservations in front of her. After all we are only ever the combination of what we believe ourselves to be and how we present ourselves to others; to have said no to Sandy that day would have marked me out – both to myself and to her – as a different person to the one I'd presented myself as for years. How could I have done that, particularly if it meant explaining the truth of how I felt?

NINE

We were at the park with quite a large group that day – all families whose children were around the same age as our own. I'd organised it, inviting the same workmate we'd met on our weekend away, a couple of families whose boys were in Marty's soccer team, a family whose daughters danced with Beccy, and another family who had children in the same class as both Beccy and Marty. Peter had even invited a work colleague and his family who had recently moved to the area.

I'd chosen that particular park because it had a BMX track, which more or less suited the age bracket of the kids. A little too easy perhaps for Marty and his friends, but on the challenging side for Beccy and hers. There was also a big playground which was useful for when the kids had enough of pedalling.

The adults had sent the kids off to play and we all sat in a big circle with the food and drink laid out in the middle. For some reason, Garry, Peter's workmate, began telling the story of how he'd met his wife, Debbie. They were both on a cruise, each with a group of friends who one night started playing a drinking game together. As well as getting blind drunk, Garry explained, he and Debbie also ended up in bed together, not even knowing each other's names the following morning – let alone what exactly it was that they'd got up to the night before.

'So our first real conversation was a pretty heavily loaded one, because we were each trying to suss the other one out about their sexual history, so we'd know how worried we should be. There was really no going back from that!' said Garry. We all laughed and Debbie raised her wine glass.

'Well, all I can say is – here's to youthful cruises and drinking games!' She lowered her voice and looked around the circle conspiratorially, 'Of course, we won't be telling the kids that story until they're at least thirty-five!'

Peter, who was sitting almost across from me, lowered his glass.

'I can remember the first time I ever saw Clair.'

I groaned and half-laughed, 'Oh no, not this story again. How much have you had to drink?'

Peter laughed. 'Yes, this story. It was at the beginning of my second year at uni. Clair was sitting in the library. She had very long hair then and she used to let it hang down on either side of her face as she studied.'

'Really? I just can't imagine Clair with long hair,' said Toni, the lady who worked with me.

I could remember, and why.

'Yes it was very long and she had this way of twisting her hair round and round her finger while she read. So for a moment I'd be able to see her face and then I couldn't. It was like watching one of those old-fashioned movies moving through frame-by-frame. I mean, she looked pretty under all that hair, but I couldn't really be sure. Let me just say that I was really distracted!'

'Well, it never took much to distract Peter from his studies!' I cut in. There was laughter all round and Peter nodded his head.

'Yes, that's true, but to be fair it was early in the year and I was still checking out all the new girls on campus. So you know, give a guy a break! Anyway, luckily for me that day the fire alarm went off. We found out later that someone had been smoking in one of the back carrels, but I can remember Clair raising her head and looking directly at me for the first time and asking me what we should do, and you know that was it. I decided there and then that I was going to marry her!'

'Of course,' I said. 'I was the third one that week he'd decided to marry.'

'Actually the fourth,' replied Peter, 'but you were the one who wanted me the most!'

Everyone laughed but me, because in a way what he said was true. I'd always known that.

Toni raised her glass, 'Well then, here's to long mysterious hair and boys who are easily distracted.'

Even I smiled at that and once again we all toasted.

Still smiling as the others began to talk amongst themselves, I rested back on one arm and looked over to where the children were riding their bikes. I saw Beccy heading up the straight of the BMX track, the streamers in her bike's handlebars bouncing up and down, her long hair flying behind her in the breeze. Beccy's bike wasn't a proper BMX, but that didn't stop her – it never had. She always powered around the track on her sparkly pink and blue bike as if her life depended on it.

Beccy had always been a determined child. I remember taking her to the beach one time when she was only two. The surf was big, the wind was blowing a gale and yet Beccy insisted on going into the water. I remember her little hand in mine, the warmth and life of it. She pulled me towards the surf with all the power of her body, urged me towards the water with the force of her mind. She was irresistible. Before I knew it, we were in the foam, goosebumps on our flesh, giggling, ducking under the water. Beccy's small body clung to mine like a baby monkey riding on its mother's back. I knew she was scared, but I also knew that she wouldn't admit to it. I've always loved that about her, the fact that she's so determined to keep up with everybody and be part of everything.

Around and around the course Beccy roared on the BMX track that day, quickly outstripping her girlfriends. As far as she was concerned they were far too slow and inexperienced for her; it was Marty and his friends she was desperate to catch and keep up with. She kept calling out to him, 'Wait for meeeeee, Marty. Wait for meeeeee.'

I could see Martin look back from time to time, caught between his friends and his sister. His legs would slow and then speed up again as he wavered between waiting for Beccy and keeping up with the other boys. Beccy's head was down, her legs pumping furiously, determination etched into her face. As she sped by where we sat, she raised her head and called out to me, 'Mum, Marty's not waiting for me!'

I nearly called out to Martin, to tell him to wait for his sister, but then I saw him slowing, the wistful look towards his friends as he let them go and he dropped back to Beccy, matching her speed as they travelled around the track together. Eventually, Marty pretended he was too tired to continue and brought Beccy over to where we all sat. She was flushed and hot, like a racing engine that's been revved to its limit, but she was happy, and as Marty walked away I caught his eye and mouthed to him 'thank you'. His smile and slight incline of his head indicated that he knew exactly what I was thanking him for. It was something I'd worked hard to teach them, brother and sister – to look out for each other. That was one of the most important lessons of all.

As I sat in the company of my husband and friends that day, watching my children play with their friends, I told myself again, as I so often did, how lucky I was; that really there was nothing in my life for me to be fearful about, nothing at all.

TEN

'*Y*ou know, I never expected it to be like this.' Sandy was in my house this time, had been invited over *after* my morning walk. I wanted to be friends with her, but needed it to be on my own terms. That's just how I was; it was my way of protecting myself. But I genuinely liked Sandy, and so I had been reckless that morning, offering her a glass of wine. She had taken it, laughing. 'Oh Clair, a glass of wine now! How am I supposed to go home and finish my housework? How am I supposed to be a good *wife* if I start to drink in the middle of a weekday? And what about you? This, this . . .' she searched for the right word as she swung her hand around, '. . . transgression. How will you ever be able to live with yourself?' She'd laughed again to show me that it was all in fun, that she meant no harm in poking fun at herself, or at me. It was what friends did, after all.

We gossiped after that, and giggled. Sandy was a natural mimic – that fact hadn't been revealed at our previous meetings – so funny at imitating the walk of the neighbour to my left, the speech of the man who owned the corner shop, that tears of laughter were running down my cheeks by the time she'd finished.

But then Sandy had become more serious. She was sitting with her body thrown back on the couch – legs crossed, pointing towards me – relaxed and at ease with herself and the world. Her fingers settled on either side of the wine glass as if she was holding a brandy snifter. I sat in one of the armchairs with my wine glass similarly in my hands and my legs tucked under me. That was when she made her comment.

'I never expected it to be like this. I never even planned to get married, you know?' she said. 'I mean, I never expected to be with a man the way that I am, let alone to be a mother living in the suburbs with a child. It's not exactly the life I planned for myself.'

I nodded at what she was saying, because it was the same for me. We were both part of the generation of women brought up to believe we could be anyone and have anything we fancied. As children we read books where doctors and astronauts were female, we watched television shows where families were blended, where roles were what we made of them. If, as a child, I'd pictured anything in my future it was myself following a successful career of some sort. For a long time I didn't believe that any man would want to marry me, and the idea of kids, while there, was like a distant blip on my radar. What I hadn't bargained for, what I hadn't even been able to imagine until it happened, was that I would love my children with a love so powerful that it made everything else redundant. How could I have known that this love would come to dominate my life? And that it could be the same for so many other women, including the one sitting opposite me?

I had to be truthful with her. 'Me either,' I admitted. 'And yet it's not such a bad life.' I looked directly at her then, almost daring her to say something different.

'Oh no, it's wonderful, it's perfect. Almost too perfect. Can anything this perfect last? Even moving to a neighbourhood like this and Chelsea meeting your kids, and Mel's, feels too good to be true sometimes. I couldn't have planned it and yet it's so . . . perfect.'

'But really,' I responded, 'this is normal. This is what normal people do.'

She laughed loudly at that. 'Wine at eleven o'clock in the morning? Oh Clair, I don't think so.' She leaned forward slightly, 'You'd better not say anything like that outside these walls – the life we have here is special, absolutely not normal.' She looked at me earnestly. 'When people, children, are starving in so many parts of the world, and when so many countries are full of war and unrest, we can't even begin to believe that what we have here is normal.'

I disagreed with her then, because I *needed* to; I *needed* to believe what I was going to say next. 'No, Sandy, we *can* have this. It just requires vigilance and will and sacrifice and a strong enough effort to keep back the rest of the world so that we can look after what we have.'

'Hmmm. I think that we can work at it, but we can't expect it. There are so many things beyond our control. Things we can't even begin to worry about. If we truly think we can control everything then we're in for a big shock one day; we're setting ourselves up for it.'

I was shaking my head at her words, agitated. I, I who had achieved so much with the sheer force of my will, I had to believe I could maintain and protect what I had. After all, what else was there? I could feel it there that day, pressing against my spine where it always sat, waiting for the right time to manifest itself, the deep-seated anxiety that was so much a part of my life: the feeling that everything I had – my husband, my children, my life – was only an illusion, that at any moment it could all be taken away from me.

Sandy, sensing something, leaned forward and rested one soft, warm hand on my leg. 'This worries you, doesn't it? Looking after your family, keeping them safe.'

Her unexpected sympathy, combined with the emotion-raising effect of the wine, was enough to blur my voice and my vision. 'It worries all of us . . . we wouldn't be very good mothers if it didn't.' I didn't want to scare her with the depth of my emotion, but I couldn't help myself.

'Of course it worries all of us, but we have to be careful Clair.' She tilted her head slightly to the side. 'We can't let it control us to the extent that it makes us useless. We won't be very good mothers if we keep second-guessing everything we do. There has to be some instinct, some spontaneity, not all worry and duty.'

I shook my head, 'No, not all duty, but a great deal of consciousness about our actions and about our role as mothers.'

Sandy leaned back in her chair again. 'Is this how you feel all the time, Clair? A constant worrying about your mothering? That must be very hard for you.'

It was too much, the blur in my eyes cleared as the tears began to fall. I leaned forward and placed my glass on the table, caught my hands between my knees and dropped my head, helpless and embarrassed at what I was revealing. Even Peter didn't know the extent of how much this concerned me, my need to protect my children far better than I had been protected – a need that made me worry about so many things. And now I was revealing all this to a woman who, in truth, I barely knew. What would she think of me?

Sandy put down her glass and came over to hug me, an unexpected, unpremeditated movement without complication or expectation. I felt the warm circle of her arms, the hint of her perfume, the soft thud of her heart. Her hug offered comfort as well as support. It was the first time in many years, probably since my mother had passed away, that I felt myself relax into the arms of another person in this way, allowed them to take some of the burden of mothering that I carried with me, always. As much as I loved my children, their hugs were not like this, they were hugging their *mother* – somebody who was the source of comfort for them, not someone who, at their age and experience anyway, could be expected to need comfort from them. And my husband had never been given any reason to expect that I needed support from him in this area.

I cried against Sandy's chest. 'Tell me about it,' she said. 'Tell me how you feel.'

'Oh Sandy, sometimes it all just seems as if it's too much. I'm the centre of it all, the last line of defence for everybody. Sometimes I don't know how I keep on doing it, even at the same time as wanting to do it. I want to look after my children and do things for them and keep them safe from the world, but sometimes it's almost too much.'

'I know, I know.' Sandy gave me a gentle squeeze. 'We have a child, or children, and it's exactly what we want, but we can't know what comes with that. We can't know that our lives will never be the same again, that our children will forever come before us, before our husbands even.' She stroked my hair. 'Don't think that I haven't thought about this as well, Clair. We couldn't ever go back to not having children, but at times the responsibility of it terrifies us.'

I was sobbing hard by then, knowing I'd be leaving mascara and make-up and mucus on Sandy's clean white shirt and yet unable to pull away. Everything she'd said was exactly what I felt but there was more, much more.

'But Clair, we can't let emotions like that completely rule our lives – second-guessing everything we do – otherwise they'd paralyse us. And, you know, in the end, no matter how much we love our children, we need to be prepared to let them go.'

I nodded against her chest and she pulled away, realising that I wanted to talk, but still she held one hand of mine, unwilling to completely give me up to myself without her support.

'You're right, of course. I know,' I snuffled, 'I know all that. It's just so hard to do it properly and even harder to find people to talk to about it. People who really understand and care. I can't even tell Peter how I feel about this.'

'Yeah, I understand. Dads love their kids in a different way to us.'

I sucked in air via my mouth, my nose too congested to breathe through. It was the first time I had ever spoken to anyone like this. I realised that this woman, Sandy, *did* understand, did *truly* understand how I felt. And despite what I had revealed to her, she hadn't dismissed me, hadn't trivialised my fears.

It was as if a lid had been lifted on something and a spring wind – full of honey and pollen and warmth – had wafted into my life, so that I could open up my lungs and breathe the lightness of a new day, a new beginning which contained within it the possibility of being free from nagging worry and tension, even if only for a time.

I had a wide circle of friends, but since my childhood I had held so many people at bay. Never, since Sharon, had I let another woman come this close, and yet, I had never considered that there was anything missing in my life.

Up until that moment.

For on that day, Sandy's gentle questioning, the press of her hand, the comfort of her hug, had shown me that what I lacked in my life were true, real, genuine friends – friends willing to ask the questions which would enable them to see the true me and who, having done so, could still accept me; who didn't always expect me to be 'calm, strong, together' Clair. Sandy had been presented to me to fill a gap in my life that I hadn't even realised was there.

I pressed back against her hand, and was opening my mouth to explain to Sandy just how important she was, when the doorbell rang.

I should have left it, but of course I could not, did not, and so I opened the door to see Mel standing there, champagne in hand. 'I hope you don't mind, sweetie,' she explained, 'but I heard voices and I don't think we've ever properly celebrated the arrival of Sandy and her family.' Mel with the sun at her back and a smile on her face; Mel who smelt of sweet perfume and unconcern. How could I not open the door and welcome her in?

And so Mel came in to share a drink with us, and if she noticed my eyes or Sandy's shirt she didn't say anything. But of course that was the way with Mel.

She was not one to ask the questions that would take her beneath life's surface.

Sandy and I were polite to Mel that day, welcomed her into the intimacy of our drinking and our conversation. But the connection had been made, that was what I thought then. Sandy would be polite to Mel, because she was polite to everyone, but it was myself and Sandy who shared a true understanding, who would become the real friends.

ELEVEN

*I*t was Marty's thirteenth birthday and, as usual, we had a cast of thousands. He was a well-liked boy, my son – invited to everyone's party and, in turn, inviting everyone to his. I didn't mind, I loved the hustle and bustle of it all. I thrived on the planning, the presents, the excitement of the children in the lead-up to the big day. I loved giving my children the most extravagant birthday parties we could afford; I always planned something that they would remember. That birthday I'd organised a pirate theme. I knew that it was probably the last year I'd get away with a themed party for Marty and I'd decided to make the most of it. To be honest, at first he wasn't happy with the idea of a party at home; he'd agitated to go to one of the laser game places which was where most of his friends held their parties. But when I reminded him that having a party at a place like that meant he'd be restricted to no more than ten guests, he decided that a party at home wasn't such a bad idea after all.

He had invited all of his soccer team, all of his cricket team, and most of the other boys in his class whether fellow sports team members or not, as well, of course, as Beccy, Tabitha, Sam and Chelsea. Our house and yard were bursting at the seams, but I loved it; I thoroughly enjoyed seeing Marty having so much fun with these friends. He played with them differently from how he played with Beccy and the neighbours; he was more grown-up, more mature, and he was extremely popular. He'd been vice-captain for the last year of primary school and had since proven to be just as well regarded at high school. His mates really got into the theme of the party. There were Jack Sparrows, Blackbeards, Bluebeards, Davy Joneses and Hooks running around everywhere. Abandoned skull-and-crossbone flags littered the lawn. Bucking the trend slightly, Beccy had dressed as Tinker Bell from *Peter Pan*. There were pirates in the *story*, she'd insisted. Sam was sporting a big black beard, which I noticed he'd absentmindedly wiped his tomato-sauce-stained hands on after eating his sausage rolls. Chelsea had come complete with a fake cutlass and Tabitha was her usual bright self, teaming her favourite red shoes with a bright red bandanna hung rakishly over one eye and a gypsy-like smock I'm sure Mel had saved from one of her pregnancies.

'Thanks Mum!' Marty said at one stage, a huge grin on his face. He was dressed as Jack Sparrow and his initially carefully applied black eyeliner had smudged and run down his cheeks with the sweat of his exertions. I knew that he was happy with his cheesy theme party, with his friends, with his mum. I reached out to wipe off the eyeliner and then grabbed him around his head holding it under my armpit until he squirmed in protest. He was growing so strong that he could have broken my grip at any time; his acquiescence was token only.

All the food for the birthday party was pirate themed, and I was dressed as Captain Hook. I'd ditched my hook, however, once I'd realised how hard it was to serve the food with only one hand. We'd played 'Walk the Plank', bobbed for apples and had an éclair-eating competition and I'd decided to allow a bit of free-play time so I could clean up before bringing out the big treasure-chest-shaped cake as a prelude to the party's end.

I was so busy shoving broken plastic cups into garbage bags, scraping cream from the deck and picking up fly-away paper plates that it was some time before I realised I didn't know where Marty was. Most of his friends were either kicking a soccer ball around or taking turns on the trampoline. But I couldn't see Marty's flamboyant pirate shirt amongst any of them. Tabby, Sam and Beccy had taken themselves away from the noise to a quiet corner of the garden where they were talking, but I could see at a glance that Marty wasn't with them. Where was he?

Dumping the garbage bags in the kitchen I did a quick circuit of the house: he wasn't in the lounge; the dining room or the bathroom. Peering out the window I could see that he wasn't in the front yard.

I moved down the corridor to the bedrooms. Beccy's door was wide open, the floor littered with discarded clothes. I could see at the end of the corridor that the door to mine and Peter's bedroom was also ajar and there wasn't anyone in there. When I came to Marty's bedroom, however, the door was firmly shut and I could hear the murmur of voices inside. More curious than anything else, I quietly turned the handle and opened the door. Marty and Chelsea were sitting cross-legged on the bed. They were side on to the door, so engrossed in each other that they didn't even realise I was there.

Marty was touching Chelsea's hair. 'It's beautiful,' I heard him say.

I stood still, not even breathing, waiting for what would come next.

Chelsea laughed. 'From my mum, that's what she told me and her mum before that. All of them had blonde hair like this. Mum told me it's the gift we give to each other. She says if I have a daughter she'll have hair just like mine.'

'So soft.' Marty's eyes were slightly glazed as if he might cry, but behind that was something else, something soft and unsullied as if he stood at the very centre of the universe and understood, for a moment, its secrets; a pure space where anything could be imagined, where his well of content was so enormous that no sacrifice was too great. It's how generations before have looked when they've considered something so perfect that it takes their breath away: the majestic immensity of St Peter's

Square in Rome; the outlook from the top of Mount Everest; the person they have fallen in love with for the very first time.

That look in Marty's eyes revealed many things: his increasing age; his changing emotions; the fact that one day he would be a man. I could accept it, I truly could, but what I could not accept was that there wasn't even a flicker in Chelsea's eyes to suggest she felt remotely the same way. What she was enjoying – purely and simply – was Marty's adoration and the power she had over him as a result of it.

'I'd do anything for you Chelsea, you know that, don't you?' Marty continued.

Chelsea laughed again, throwing her head back so that her hair rippled down her back. 'I know. And one day you might have to.'

It was in that moment when her eyes met mine in the mirror above Marty's bed, her lips curled in a triumphant smile, that I understood: Chelsea had enticed my son in here, away from his friends, so that she could enjoy every ounce of the power she knew she possessed over him. Even in her youth, she was one of the most dangerous females I had ever met.

Quietly I closed the door, my own lips pressed into a tight line as I called to everyone, Martin and Chelsea included, that it was cake time. But that party, that day, was when I really began to wonder, just exactly where this was going to take us all.

TWELVE

*I*t was late Saturday afternoon and Peter was due home in a couple of hours. He'd been away all week and would manage to make it home just in time to see us all for the last bit of the weekend before heading off again on another week-long trip on Monday. He didn't always work as hard as this, but when he did we all missed him, me in particular. The day was warm and we'd been out all morning. There was a peace about the house; morning activities and jobs done. The afternoon was well advanced and all of us were looking forward to Peter's return. The children were settled in front of the television and I was taking a short nap in my room. It was while I was lying down that I heard the laughter from Mel's. It was a trick of acoustics: anything that was said on her back deck was somehow concentrated against my corner window – indented in some cute architect's trick, a furnishing nightmare – and then amplified and funnelled into my room as if I was standing right next to the speaker. I had often wondered if there was an obligation on me to mention the effect to Mel, but had never been entirely sure how and when to tell her: after the first time I'd heard her and Joe fighting? The morning I'd heard her talking on the phone when her sister had rung to tell her of the death of their mother? No, the time had never seemed entirely right and I'd let it go.

So I heard the laughter and voices that day, but at first couldn't be sure who was speaking.

Standing, I tiptoed to the window and opened it a fraction to better hear what was going on. I heard Mel offering drinks; I heard someone replying in a low voice – Sandy! I heard David and Joe laughing together. There was the clink of glasses. The children began a game which seemed to involve running around the house chasing each other. It was Sandy and her family, over at Mel's.

I stood against the window urging myself to lie down again and that was when I sensed, rather than heard, the door to my room opening a crack. It was Beccy; no time to return to my bed.

'Mummy, what're you doing?'

'Oh nothing darling, I was just a bit hot, that's all. I thought I'd open the window a bit.'

Beccy came and stood beside me. 'What are they doing out there? They're making a lot of noise.'

'I know darling.' I moved towards the bed. 'Why don't you come and rest with me.' I didn't know whether voices travelled in the other direction as well, and wasn't keen for it to be known that I was listening in.

Beccy opened the window a bit wider. 'But what are they doing, Mummy? Is that Chelsea over there with them?' She leaned forward to see better and I was sure she was about to yell out.

'Beccy, close that window and come over here with me now,' I hissed at her.

She looked at me wonderingly for a moment but then slid the window shut and obediently came over to me. It was too late, however; I'd heard Marty's footsteps on the back deck. 'Hey, you guys, what're you up to?' He was yelling to make himself heard over the squealing. The children stopped running to answer him, but I could still hear them giggling.

'Mummy, can I go out?' Beccy whispered.

'No, stay here.'

'Just playing.' It was Tabby answering Martin's question.

'What?'

'Not much, just running. What're you doing?'

'Just watching TV.'

'What're you watching?'

'Oh, nothing much. Is your mum over there as well Chels?'

'Yeah, and my dad. We're having a Bar Be Cue.' Each syllable carefully separated and enunciated.

'Oh, right.'

There was more giggling. 'Do you want to come over and play?' It was Sam. I heard the sound of someone slapping someone else on the arm.

'Don't be silly,' Chelsea said. 'We're going to have dinner soon and they haven't been invited.' Her voice had a cruel lilt to it and I remembered her smile at Marty's party.

'Mummy, can I go out?' Beccy was squirming now, but I had a very firm hold on her arm. She wasn't going anywhere. I wanted to hear how this ended.

'He can still come over,' Sam said.

'Well, not really,' said Tabitha. 'I mean Chelsea's right. We're having dinner and it's just us. I mean it's a kind of *formal* thing.'

'Why can't he come under the fence? He can go home when dinner's ready.'

'Yeah, I could come under the fence. That's what I always do. It's not exactly as if you could stop me.'

There was whispered conferring on the other side of the fence.

'Well Chelsea says I *could* stop you if I wanted to,' replied Tabitha. 'I mean it *is* our land; if you came over without asking that would be trespassers.' More whispering. 'Trespassing, I mean.'

It was Chelsea again, whispering into Tabitha's ear, telling her what to say. After Martin had told her exactly how he felt about her at his birthday party; after he had made himself vulnerable to her . . . this was how she was treating him.

'But I always go over to your side,' Martin protested.

'Yes, but that's when she wants you to,' Chelsea's voice rang out.

'So don't you want me to come over now?'

'It's not that,' replied Tabitha. 'It's just that we're going to have dinner soon and I'm not sure if your mum would let you come over anyway.'

'Tabby, Sam, Chelsea. Come and have something to drink before dinner.' I heard Mel's voice call out in a sing-song way. There was no sound of movement from the kids, but then I heard footsteps as Mel walked over to the edge of her deck. '*There* you all are. Oh hello, Marty, how're you going? Is your dad home yet?'

'No, not yet.'

'He's coming home today, isn't he?'

'Yeah.'

'That's what I thought.'

There was a pause and then Martin's voice again. 'Mel?'

'Yes, sweetie?'

'I was wondering, if Mum says it's okay, can we come over and play as well?'

'Well, if your dad's coming home soon maybe it's not such a good idea. I mean your mum might want you to be home when he arrives.'

'But he'll know where we are and we can look out for him and when we see him we can come back.'

There was a beat of silence and then, 'Sure Marty, that's fine with me, so if you think it's okay ask your mum, sweetie. If she says it's fine, you're more than welcome to come over and have dinner with us – your mum as well. I've got heaps of food.'

'Hang on, I'll ask her. MUUUUUM.' Marty was already calling out to me as he walked off the deck. I put one hand over Beccy's mouth. I didn't want anyone to know I was sitting, listening.

With Beccy firmly clutched to my side I moved into the corridor. 'Yes,' I called out. Martin was just pushing his way into the corridor as well.

'Mum, is it okay if we go over next door for dinner? Mel just invited us.'

'Oh did she darling? That's nice of her, but you know that Daddy's coming home soon.'

'But Mum, why can't we go over until he gets here? He'll know where we are.'

'Oh Martin, really we should stay here. I've got something really nice ready for our dinner tonight.'

Beccy was glaring at me. 'Mum! Why can't we go over? We go over all the time! AND we've been invited, so why not?'

I turned to Martin. 'Marty will you go outside and say thank you very much to Mel, but that we won't be coming over. And then I want you to come down to the lounge room. Beccy and I will be waiting for you there.'

Obediently, Martin went outside, did what I asked and then came to where Beccy and I sat in the lounge.

Martin looked very unhappy: his forehead creased, his eyebrows lowered. 'Why can't we go over Mum? She invited us.'

'Yes, she invited you now, as an afterthought. We weren't invited in the first place which is why we're not going.'

'But Mum, when I went outside just now, Mel told me she hadn't invited us because she thought Dad was coming home soon and that we'd want to spend some time with him.'

I sighed. 'Okay, look that's probably true. Mel's a thoughtful neighbour. The truth, Marty, is that I don't want any of us going over there after the way Chelsea spoke to you – saying that if you went through the fence it'd be trespassing!'

'That was Tabitha, Mum.'

'Yes, with Chelsea telling her what to say!'

Martin shook his head, 'No, I don't think so. It was Tab who said it anyway.'

It was my turn to shake my head, 'No, the reality is that Chelsea wasn't very nice to you and Tabitha was carried along with her. They can't be allowed to speak to you like that, to bully you like that. You can't let people push you around, Marty, which is the real reason we're not going over there tonight and that's all there is to it. Come on, let's go and whip the cream for dessert. I've made Dad's favourite apple pie.'

A few days later, I heard laughter coming from Sandy's house. She and Mel were sitting in the shade on the back deck, laughing, sharing a drink. First the two families' children ganged up against Marty and now the women were enjoying each other's company – without me. I sighed, feeling the heavy weight of my heart within my chest. It's what I should have expected, I supposed, that Sandy would enjoy the company of the ever-laughing Mel more than she would enjoy mine. How could I really have expected anything else?

THIRTEEN

*S*ummer, and like an unfurling fern frond I felt my body unclenching. Perhaps it was the heat, or the fact I wasn't tied to the daily schedule of school lunches, school notes and after-school activities. But things seemed to be worrying me less; even Chelsea's near-constant presence didn't irritate me as much as previously and her behaviour towards Marty seemed to have improved, even though I still didn't completely like or trust her.

Peter was around more than usual as well. It was a quiet work period for him and he often came home early. We had taken to barbecuing on the back deck. Sometimes the other families would do the same and the three groups of us would be eating at the same time, the children scoffing their food as fast as possible so they could slip through the fences and play in whichever yard took their fancy that evening. Sometimes the adults would come together for a meal or for drinks before or afterwards, but often we did not. At the time I thought I was learning to truly relax: to expect very little from anyone or anything; to be happy with what I had and what was freely given to me.

The word that came to my mind on more than one occasion that summer was 'halcyon'. I'd looked it up in the dictionary years ago after I saw a house for sale with that same name – Halcyon. It was an old word, originally describing a mythical bird with powers to calm the wind and the waves so that the ocean was peaceful during its breeding season over the winter solstice. From this, the word had come to mean a period of peace, calm and prosperity when the pressures of the world were held at bay. This was how I felt that summer: calm and at peace. Dangerous, dangerous, dangerous. It's always at times like this that you are taken unaware.

One night, the children in bed, so hot that I lay naked on the covers, windows open to catch any breeze that must be coming – soon – moonlight through the leaves. My husband, fresh from the shower, wet hair plastered to his scalp, so short and so fair that he was young again and so was I, remembering how I had felt about him in the early days of our relationship when anything, absolutely anything was possible with our lives, a feeling so powerful, so poignantly reminiscent of who I once was, who we once were – before the tethering with age, and responsibility and mortgage and children – that I felt as if I would cry. The great welling within my chest for a life and a relationship which once had seemed so perfect, and so perfectly poised, that it could go any way, would be able to crash through any barrier with the momentum of its own power.

Peter stood over me, looking down at my body with a desire that was also young and full of infinite promise. There was nothing between us that night but the tidal pull of our lust pushing all before us, tiredness and age and subtle discontent, so that we were washed clean and ready and waiting for whatever would be coming to us. It was as if a film had been removed from the world and everything was reduced to essence, clear and bright and simple, able to be touched – nothing between me and it, nothing between me and him.

He reached down, touching my body with his fingers and then with his mouth, the warm trickle of heated breath contracting my desire to this point and then that, following the tracking of his lips, so that everywhere else on my body suddenly seemed cool in comparison. And then, his tongue was licking my body from the base of my belly to the base of my neck, my body arching in anticipation of where, just where, he would touch me next. It was minutes or hours, a dreamscape of time, until I could not take anymore and I sat up, his saliva cooling on my body as I took him into my mouth where he stood, my hands gripped hard into his buttocks so that he could not escape.

He was moaning then and his pleasure was mine. It was so, so long since I'd done this to him, my life now so far removed from the early years of naked sleep, and hands and mouths groping in the dark for another body that was, also, free and insatiable. How had it happened? The dropping away of the need and the desire, still there perhaps, but dampened by duty and necessity – the early meeting, the late night, the paths that did not pass with such easy familiarity, the bodies and the needs of the children that came between. Welcome, but an intrusion nevertheless. How had it happened?

For that moment I couldn't imagine how I'd lived without this. His pleasure, my pleasure – there was no barrier between the two.

Pulling him out of my mouth just before he came, the fountaining on my body, the cooling of his fluid, and his hands and tongue between my legs. Just as I liked it, just as I liked it. A dissolving into sensation that allowed no other intrusion into my head beyond the physical; a blessed, blessed relief from all that usually bound me. And that night there was the sleep, deep and long, bodies intertwined like first-time lovers.

I was careless with my peace that night, used it to merge into my husband, manipulated it to sink into the oblivion of sleep. If only I had known what was to come, I would have clung to those moments, drawn them out to last for all eternity.

In the end, however, it was probably lucky I hadn't. How could any of us bear to know what is to come?

FOURTEEN

It was almost at the end of that long, wonderful summer holiday. The children had played together every day the week before. The obligations of the early part of the holidays – the summer camps, the sleepovers with other friends – had been fulfilled and now we were all in proper holiday mode. The children's play had settled into an easy rhythm; even Chelsea was less demanding and bossy than usual. Sometimes the kids ate together, at whichever house they happened to be, but that day I'd decided to call my children home for lunch. I wanted to prepare a proper meal for them, with salad and fruit, easier to accomplish with my kids on their own.

It wasn't yet time to eat, but I decided to take a look at what they were up to outside and so I saw almost all of it. Would it have been different if I hadn't witnessed what happened? Would I have understood things differently? Who really knows; things are as they are.

They were playing on the swing that morning. Over time I'd almost become inured to its dangers. I still didn't like to watch Beccy using it. I usually went inside or turned away when it was her turn, but I reasoned that my kids getting a bit of excitement with a swing I could at least see, was better than them looking for excitement further away from our home. I believed then that there are degrees of safety; that by keeping those I loved close to me, by watching all they did, I could keep them safe. I was naïve. I should have remembered that disaster can strike anyone, at any time, in any place.

An incident from the night before had prompted me to go outside to check on the children that morning. Beccy had been playing with her dinner – very unlike her usual self – and I'd asked her what the matter was. She hadn't answered, but Martin had, putting his knife and fork carefully down on his plate before replying. 'She had a bit of a fight with Chelsea.'

This wasn't unusual. Despite Beccy's loyalty to the girl she called her 'best friend', despite my almost-acceptance of her in my house, in our lives, I knew that Chelsea still wasn't always as nice to my daughter as she could have been.

'So what happened?' I asked. 'Was this fight worse than usual?'

Again Beccy didn't answer, but Martin nodded. 'Yeah. But it was kind of Beccy's fault.'

'How?'

'Well . . .'

It was obvious that Martin was reluctant to say more, but where my kids are concerned I don't mind pushing. 'Tell me, Martin,' I ordered.

'Well, Beccy wanted everyone to play statues, but no-one else wanted to, so Beccy said she'd cry and go inside and tell you unless everyone did what she wanted.'

'I didn't say that, Marty.' Beccy's arms were folded firmly across her body.

'You did, Beccy. You know you did.'

'Did not.'

I broke in. 'Did everyone not want to play Beccy's game, Martin, or was it just Chelsea?'

'Nobody really wanted to play, but we didn't know what else to play either.'

'Because you know, Martin, that I expect you to stand up for your sister when someone's not being nice to her.' It was something I told the children over and over: they would have lots of friends in their lives, but they would never have another brother or sister.

'I do stick up for her, Mum. I stick up for her *all* the time. And like I said no-one wanted to play statues, but we probably would have anyway, like we usually do, except that when Beccy said she'd go and tell you, Chelsea got really angry.'

'Yeah, Mummy, and she said something about you that wasn't very nice and that's what made *me* really sad – and a bit angry.'

'She said something about me?' I was surprised by this, even though I probably shouldn't have been. Girls like Chelsea thrive on power and fear: obviously picking only on Beccy personally wasn't working well enough for her. So she'd decided to see if she could upset Beccy by targeting me as well. 'What exactly did she say?'

'That you worry about everything and that you always take Beccy's side.'

'She called you a control freak, Mummy.'

'Really, did she?' I examined my reactions and was surprised at how unruffled I felt.

'Yeah.' Now that Beccy had decided to tell me what happened, she wasn't inclined to stop. 'She said that you were bossy and then she laughed at you, and at us.'

'How?'

'She said you always had to know where we were and that you never let us go anywhere by ourselves.'

'That bit is kinda true,' mumbled Marty.

'Thank you, Martin! There's nothing wrong with me knowing where you are.'

He shrugged.

I turned to Beccy. 'Is that all she said, because, you know, that's really not so bad. It sounds a bit to me like she's jealous of you and Marty because her mum doesn't look after her the same way I look after you.'

'I don't think she's jealous of us, Mummy. I think she thinks that we're silly.' Beccy looked as if she might cry.

'What do you mean?'

'Like babies who can't look after ourselves. She called me a baby, Mummy. She said I always go crying to you and that I'm too scared to go as high on the swing as everyone else. So I got on the swing and Chelsea pushed me so high that I got scared and had to tell her to stop. Chelsea said I wouldn't be allowed on the swing anymore. She said she'd find all my school friends and tell them I'm a baby.'

I held Beccy's hand in mine. I felt surprisingly calm about what she'd told me, but still I knew that she both expected and needed my support on this. 'Look darling,' I said. 'Look, both of you. I know that you both like Chelsea.'

Beccy shook her head and pouted, 'Not anymore.'

'Well, perhaps in one way that's good. Because fundamentally Chelsea is a bully. She likes, *needs* maybe, to have power over people. She's a spoiled child, completely used to getting what she wants. That makes her a bully. She's tried to hurt you Beccy, to hurt me and Marty as well. But she hasn't, and you must never, never allow bullies to hurt you. You too, Marty. I want you both to remember that. The only way to deal with bullies is to stand up to them, to make them afraid of you. Do you understand what I'm saying?'

Both Marty and Beccy nodded.

'So Beccy, you mustn't let Chelsea get away with anything like that ever again, and you, Martin, you must make sure that you look after your sister and support her. I know how you feel about Chelsea, that you think she's a good friend of yours, but Beccy is your sister and *she's* the one you have to look after. Do you understand what I'm saying?'

They both nodded again, and that, I'd believed, would be that. My children were armed; they would be able to deal with whatever Chelsea could throw at them. I was quietly happy with myself that night. I'd prepared my children far better to deal with life than I'd ever been prepared by my own mother.

So perhaps it was the incident from the night before, which had been playing in the back of my mind, that took me out onto the deck that morning. Perhaps I simply wanted to see if my previous night's words had any effect on Beccy's behaviour. Whatever the reason, the fact is that I was on the deck the moment it happened; I saw it all.

FIFTEEN

*I*t is noisy over there, but it often is. It's as if the children are all talking over the top of each other. There's yelling, but I can't make out what's being said. The voices are unusually loud; I think that the children may be arguing.

Chelsea is on the swing. She's swinging steadily higher and higher. I see that Beccy is trying to help, to push Chelsea in her lower back before she streams back up again. As Chelsea swings higher and faster Beccy is having more and more trouble reaching her. Most of the time Beccy misses completely, but then, just as Chelsea goes higher than she has before, just as she comes down faster than she has before, instead of touching her properly, in the small of her back, Beccy appears to push awkwardly, unusually hard against the seat of the swing, so that Chelsea's body seems to slide backwards. For a time she is still almost 'sitting' on the swing on the back of her knees, but as the swing continues higher, she slips further so that she is hanging only by her ankles, although her hands still grip the ropes. That is when Marty jumps, catching the edge of the swing's seat with his strong right hand. The swing stops hard, with a jerk. Looking down at him, at all the other children, eyes wide, Chelsea loses her grip and falls to the ground just below the highest point of the swing's trajectory.

These are moments suspended in time, I will return to them again and again, these actions, to the possible intent behind them. I cannot be sure, I will never truly be sure exactly what it was I saw in those moments, and I already know that it's something I'll never be able to discuss directly with my children – or with Peter. But my words from the night before echo in my head, even in those first seconds of held breath when I hope that everything will be all right: *'The only way to deal with bullies is to stand up to them, to make them afraid of you.'* That's what I'd told my children and they'd nodded, as if they truly understood, as I wanted them to.

I can't see where, or how, Chelsea has fallen. It's possible she's all right, a lesson learned, but largely unharmed; I tell myself that at any moment I'll see her head over the top of the fence as she dusts herself down and complains about what's happened. For a while I watch, too long; I watch until the screaming begins.

Dropping the tea towel I'd been holding from my hands, I run to the edge of the deck and down the stairs. The screaming has stopped and I hear voices, one raised above the others. It's Martin who's speaking the loudest, shouting urgently over the children until they're forced to listen to him, but I can't hear what he's saying. As I run, I begin to call for Sandy. I don't know if she's seen or heard what's just happened. It will take too long for me to go around to her yard via the street and I think that I will, just, be able to fit under the fence. I get down on my hands and knees and it's as if my very world has been tilted. I've lowered myself to the size of the children. For a moment the world is full of contrast: the trees above look awfully big; the sky infinite. At the same time, however, I see every blade of grass up close, feel the moisture of the ground begin to seep through the knees of my jeans, smell the damp loam. It's so long since I've been this close to the earth and it's as if everything has changed. There's a freshness about the universe, a clarity in being this close to everything, as if life is not as complicated as it usually is, as if the possibilities are endless. The broken palings of the fence scrape against my skin as I push my way underneath and I don't even realise that a splinter of wood has embedded itself in the top of my neck. It will be removed later that terrible night by Peter, carefully, with tweezers and steady hands.

Standing up on the other side of the fence, stretched to my full height, the world falls into place again, water returning to its correct level, and the moment of peace which I felt under the fence, at the level of the children, in the space of transition from one place to another, disappears; I realise what I now have to face, and with that comes the beginning of the true fear.

Chelsea's head is at a funny angle, a strange, out-of-place dent on the right side of her skull. I can see that she's been thrown against one of the raised roots of the tree; a small deviation to the left or right and things would have been different. I pick up her hand. She is very warm, her body with a light film of sweat from summer and her exertions. I twist her arm slightly to feel for a pulse. There isn't one.

That's when I look up and see Sandy coming towards us. Her face has dissolved, as if someone has thrown acid on her, features blurring into one another in an almost exaggerated mask of horror. She is not speaking, perhaps she is unable to, but her expression is enough to tell me everything. Sandy knows exactly what has happened to her only child. I feel my heart leave my body and wrap itself around her, wanting to push her back to save her from all that is to come, but she is not to be halted, there is absolutely nothing that I can do to shield her from the devastation of this. I know that it's already too late for her, but perhaps I can save my children from the enormity of what they've done, from the dark place where my words of last night directed them.

Before Sandy reaches us, I turn to the children. I speak low and urgently, my eyes and my tone willing them to obey me.

'Go inside all of you, to our house. Martin ring triple 0, ask for the ambulance, give them Chelsea's address, tell them to get here quickly. There's no need to say any more than that. We'll talk to them when they arrive.'

The children move in a wave, like migratory birds, ducking under the fence and into the sanctuary of the house. Then Sandy is beside me, bending down to her daughter, taking Chelsea into her arms, arms that can no longer offer safety or comfort. It is the worst thing that can happen to a mother, to be denied that ability to care properly for her child. Sandy is still and silent, a deadly silence.

'Oh Sandy,' I say. I place one arm around her shoulders. 'I've sent the children in to ring for an ambulance.'

'It's too late.' Her voice is muffled against the body of her daughter, the extent of her grief revealed only in the tremors that course through her body.

'Yes.' There's nothing I can do but agree. 'I . . . I don't know what happened. Did you see it?'

Silence from Sandy; an eternity of silence.

I try again. 'I was inside. I stepped outside just as I heard the screaming, but I didn't see what happened. Did you?'

This time she shakes her head. 'No, I didn't see it, but I know what happened. I know she fell from this dreadful swing. The swing she insisted on having. The swing neither of us could deny her. If only we'd been stronger; if only we'd said "no" to her!' Sandy is crying silently, desperately.

There is nothing more for me to say. I stay there with her, while she holds her child and I hold her, until the ambulance comes. By that time the children have returned and they stand around us, watching, guarding. At one point I look over to where Marty stands and I see the look on my son's face: shock, fear, a closed wariness. My eyes follow Marty's arm down to where his hand grips Beccy's hand, hard, her hand pressing back, and I know that at least my children are doing as I have always told them: they have closed ranks; they are protecting each other.

SIXTEEN

I take my children home, the correct way this time, away from that house, up the straight of the street, then left at the corner and left again to our home. No more ducking under the fence, not for now, and probably not forever. I lock the door, order the children to sit on the couch, tell them not to move while I make myself a cup of tea. I know it won't be long before they are interviewed, before they will be expected to answer questions; I know that there are things I must prepare them for, but first I must prepare myself.

I move around the kitchen, my hands shaking as I fill the kettle, tip the tea into the infuser. I know that what I witnessed that morning from my back deck was enough for a strong case to be made that my children have acted maliciously, or at the very least carelessly. I am, of course, concerned about the legal ramifications of what my children have done, but it is the emotional consequences for them, the effect on the rest of their lives – if their guilt is ever brought home to them, if they are ever allowed to admit and dwell on the enormity of what they have done – that truly terrifies me. Because I also know that no-one, apart from me, could ever understand their actions or their motivations. No-one else could truly understand that what my children did was not a simple, unprovoked act, that it had a trail leading back to the very first day when the new family moved in behind us; the day when Chelsea's father hung that swing; the days following when friendships were forged and tested. I always knew that Chelsea, with her blonde hair and engaging ways, was a dangerous, deceptive child, a potential threat to my children and my carefully constructed life. Now I needed to consider what must be done next; how best to protect my children from the consequences of their actions.

I crouch in front of them now, holding each of my children by an arm, just above the elbow, leaning in so close that I'm unable to see the two of them at once, having to turn my head, first to one and then to the other as I speak to them. I know that I should be consoling them, but first there is this to do, to get through. I have no other choice.

'I saw what happened,' I say, my voice low and urgent. 'I know that it was an accident, only an accident.'

I wait until both Marty and Beccy nod. Beccy begins to squirm, 'You're hurting my arm, Mummy.' I ignore her. It's true that my grip is a little tight, but I'm not about to loosen it just yet, perhaps not for a long time yet.

'That's all you have to tell the police when they come to talk to you, that what happened was an accident. The police mightn't be very nice, they might ask hard questions, but that's all you need to tell them, that Chelsea fell backwards and that it was an accident; that she always went too high on the swing. Do you understand?' I realise that I've begun to shake my children slightly; their bodies jerk awkwardly, puppets with broken strings.

Beccy begins to cry. 'You're hurting me, Mummy, *and* you're scaring me.'

Marty is scowling. 'Of course that's what we're going to tell them, Mum. Do you think we're stupid or something? Of course that's what happened and of course that's what we're going to tell them, all of us. We all know what to say; we've all agreed. It was an accident.'

I almost sag in relief at his words, at the realisation that Marty has already thought this through and decided on a course of action that agrees with my own. I hadn't realised how much my concern for my children had been keeping me upright. Letting go of their arms I lean over and give Beccy a hug, eyes closed, chin resting against my daughter's head. 'It's okay darling, it's okay. I'll make sure that everything will be okay.'

I feel Marty move, and opening my eyes I see that he is still scowling, looking directly at me.

'How can it be okay, Mum? Chelsea's dead. Accident or not. How can it be okay? *Nothing's* okay.' He pulls himself off the couch, away from my outstretched arm, and leaves the room.

Sandy's on the phone, the line is clear, but her voice sounds distant as if she's trying to recall herself from somewhere far away. 'I'm sorry,' she says. 'I had to call to tell you . . . the police want to speak to your children and to Mel's. I told them that the kids'd be very upset, that I could tell them what happened and that I really would prefer it if the children didn't have to talk to them. But they said they'd have to speak to all the children who were here today. I'm going to ring Mel in a minute and tell her as well. I think they'll be coming round tomorrow morning, early. I just wanted to let you know.'

'That's okay, Sandy.' I reply. 'Look, let me ring Mel for you. This isn't something you should have to do. I'll get her to bring her kids round here in the morning. She can spend some time with you, and the police can interview the kids together.'

'No, no that's okay, I really should do it. I'll talk to her.'

'No,' I insist, 'I'll do it. Let me take care of some things for you.'

There is a moment of silence and then a voice filled with a small measure of relief. 'Thank you, Clair, thank you for this, and for everything.'

The following morning, I sit Tabitha, Sam and my children down together. Mel has asked me to call her when the police come, but I want this time to talk with the children first. They all look tired; faces pale, eyes red-rimmed. I don't know about Tabby and Sam, but I know that my children slept fitfully last night. I went in to Beccy many times, replacing her covers, offering her a hug, a drink of water. This has been easy for no-one, *will* be easy for no-one.

'Okay,' I begin, 'some policemen will be coming soon. They'll want to know exactly what happened yesterday with Chelsea. Apparently they have to prepare something to give to a person who is called the Coroner. The Coroner will be the one to decide what actually caused Chelsea's death and how it happened.'

'What do you mean?' asks Tabitha. Her feet are drawn up under her and her hands are tucked into her armpits; she has rounded her body into a tight ball.

'Well, it looks like Chelsea died because she hit her head, but maybe there was something that happened before that . . .' I shrug as if I am very casual, but I'm being careful with what I say today. I know that I scared Martin and Beccy with my questioning yesterday and I don't want to do that now. 'You know, she might have had a heart attack or something and that made her fall off the swing.'

'Did Chelsea have a heart attack?' asks Sam. His already small eyes are almost squeezed shut, swollen from crying and probably lack of sleep. 'Is that what happened to her? I thought . . .' He looks around at the others obviously confused and distraught and I hasten to reassure him.

'No,' I try to speak in a calm voice. 'I'm not saying that. I'm just explaining that what looks obvious to us might not actually be clear to other people. The police will ask you questions so that they can try to understand what happened to Chelsea.'

'But we all know what happened,' says Marty, his eyes darting round the other children. 'It was an accident. She was swinging too high. We've all been told not to swing that high and she slipped and fell off.'

'That's right,' says Tabitha. She is rocking herself back and forwards, her bottom acting as a fulcrum. 'We've all been told that. Chelsea knew that.'

'I tried to catch her,' says Beccy, 'but she was going too high and too fast.' She begins to cry; Tabitha stops her rocking and uncurls herself, placing an arm around my daughter's shoulders.

'So Beccy, you didn't touch the swing at all while Chelsea was swinging?' I look at all the children, then press ahead without waiting for Beccy's answer. 'Did anyone touch the swing?' I know that this is potentially a dangerous question to ask, but I want to know the answer to it now – after all, it's something the police are likely to ask as well.

Beccy opens her mouth as if to say something, but Tabitha gets in before her. 'Nobody touched the swing,' she says shaking her head, a note of finality in her voice.

Sam looks at the other children and then speaks. 'Maybe Chelsea had on slippery pants. Maybe that's why she slipped.' He nods his head up and down. 'I didn't like using that swing when I was wearing my special tennis pants,' he adds.

I know the ones Sam is talking about; they are a synthetic 'parachute silk', the type of material my children always liked to wear to the park when they were younger so they could plummet ever faster down the slippery slide.

'What was Chelsea wearing yesterday?' I ask. I can't remember; there's nothing I can recall of the girl from yesterday, nothing apart from the shocked, immovable face, the neck bent at a strange angle.

There's silence while the children think. 'Actually,' says Tabitha, 'she had on a skirt, but I think she might have been wearing her shiny gym pants underneath.' Her voice trails off. 'I didn't think about that.'

'You see? These are the type of things you need to tell the police,' I say. 'All these little details will help them understand what happened.'

Again it is Tabitha who speaks; she is also crying now, the tears running down her cheeks. 'We were all talking to each other, you know, like usual. We thought we were having fun and playing, that it was a game like any other time.' She looks at the others. 'Didn't we?' Everybody nods.

'But it wasn't,' adds Martin, looking down at his hands. He is sitting on an armchair, a little removed from the other children, and he seems terribly alone. 'It wasn't a game like any other time, because this time Chelsea died.'

Later, as I am in the kitchen preparing a snack for the children, I take a peek at them waiting in the lounge. I feel some relief after my conversation with them; the police will come, but it will be all right, the children are up to whatever will be asked of them. Marty has moved to the couch with the others. He has put his arm around Beccy and I see her rest against him and then the other children move in close as well. They huddle like that as if in that small warmth, the press of bodies, they will find comfort. I feel so sorry for them, because I know that all they will find instead, all they will feel, is the space, the absence, the deep empty loneliness of a lost friend. I am sorry for them, so deeply sorry for them, for what has happened, for what is to come.

SEVENTEEN

I've experienced the loss of a friend, so I know how my children feel. The difference is that my friend didn't die; she simply chose to leave me. And I never really knew why. I still don't. At first I'd believed myself unworthy of her friendship, unworthy of anyone's friendship; later I realised that nothing is ever that simple, that you need to be willing to take responsibility for how some things in your life unfold.

It was at that awkward time of my life, of everyone's life perhaps – my first year of high school when I was no longer a child, but not yet a teenager; when early interactions have the power to shape the rest of your high school days. Sharon was the only real friend I had; the one girl I liked from primary school who had gone on to attend the same high school as me. I'd been bullied in primary school and had found it hard to make friends: a little too lacking in confidence; a little too tall; a little different in subtle ways. The nuances of childhood likes and dislikes are not always obvious.

Maybe I clung too hard to Sharon; in fact I know that I clung too hard. She was the one I sat with at lunchtime, walked home with, rang on the phone when I was allowed to. She was my one line of defence against the world and one day she crumbled. I came out of my classroom for recess and there she was, sitting with another group, some girls from her English class. When I went to join them, they turned away from me, would not include me in their circle. I saw the look on Sharon's face that day: relief, triumph – she'd managed to distance herself from me, had been accepted by others, and for her there would be no turning back. I'd felt everything drain away from me then, the last vestiges of my confidence pooling at my feet.

What happens when you're in your first year of high school and there's no-one to sit with at lunchtime, no-one to whisper to during classes?

I'll tell you what happens: you become vulnerable, marked as easy prey. And so you become a ghost, shrivelling yourself almost into invisibility in the hope that no-one will see or bother with you. Sharon had set me up for that and yet I still missed her, still would have been her friend if she had asked me to. And what's worse, she became my nemesis, perhaps so desperate to prove her distance from me that she had to become cruel. She wouldn't allow me to disappear, was the one who made fun of me most of all: standing at the school gate waiting for me when I arrived; meeting me around a corner to comment on my legs, my hair, my lack of friends.

There was one day, I remember well. It was my birthday and no-one at school remembered, or cared – except Sharon. 'Having a party?' she'd asked as I walked in that morning. 'Oh that's right, you've got no friends who'd come!' Turning then to her new admirers so they could appreciate her wit. They'd all laughed, bonding over the misery of another. It had gone on all day, the relentless teasing that made me sink in my seat and seek the furthest reaches of the playground to eat my lunch, alone.

I was on my way home that afternoon when I had to pass Sharon, standing on the train platform, surrounded by the school's cool kids. I tried to slink past, but she saw me. 'How ya goin', Birthday Girl? Going home to your mummy and daddy to blow out your candles by yourself?' she called. The other kids turned to look at me, their faces lit with laughter – laughing at me, at my friendlessness, at my powerlessness.

I slunk away then, moved closer to the tunnel through which trains approached the station, hiding myself in the shadows of the station building's overhang – inadequate in summer, inadequate in the rain and inadequate then to conceal the depth of my embarrassment. I remember removing the tie that bound my hair and shaking my head so that my face was obscured. Then I took a book from my bag and held it up high in front of me to complete my camouflage. At first I pretended to read, but then I actually did read, until the background reality of the sun-baked platform shrank into an out-of-focus haze around me. I looked up from my book ten minutes later, or was it twenty? I had so lost myself that I wasn't even sure if my train had come or gone and I didn't really care. There was no way I was going near Sharon and her friends again.

But that was when I saw Sharon was alone; she and I completely alone on the platform. For a moment, as she looked around, her eyes caught mine and, in an old reflex of complicity, I smiled. What did I expect from her? I wonder that even now. For from her at that moment there was nothing, not even a glimmer of acknowledgement. It was as if I no longer existed in her world. She turned her blank eyes away from me and faced towards the tracks, her head down as she began to trace one foot along the yellow line marking the edge of the platform's safe area. Obviously, with no audience present, I was so insignificant that I wasn't even worth the bother of her derision.

At that thought I began to shake; shivers I couldn't control racked my body. I realised then that I was completely disposable, every vestige of my self-image had been stripped away by the girl who stood in front of me.

I felt the slight movement of air through the tunnel that always preceded even the sound of a train approaching the station. I breathed deeply, closed my book and put it into my bag, observing the trembling of my hands as I did so. I wondered if that trembling would ever stop.

My mind was blank as I began to move up behind Sharon.

In the days when we'd been friends I'd liked to sneak up behind her, put my hands over her eyes and ask her to guess who it was. When we were friends it had been a game, but that day on the platform it wasn't.

I was very quiet. It was only when really it should have been too late, when I stood directly behind her, my mouth close enough for my breath to blow the hairs on the back of her neck – with no-one as a witness and the train almost upon us – when I could have said and done anything to her that I wanted to, that she half-turned to me, and I saw the shudder of disgust that moved across her face. I stopped at that; could go no further.

Of course I was unable to act in order to protect myself from her. How could I have asserted myself then – particularly in the face of her judgement of me – when all my life I had been taught the opposite?

Throughout primary school, my mother had discouraged assertiveness of any form. 'What would people think of you?' she'd say. 'Turn the other cheek. Don't lower yourself to their level.' Those words made me feel I was only as good as somebody else's regard; those words meant I had never acted to protect myself from anything; those words had made me so dependent on Sharon's friendship, so vulnerable when she turned against me and so incapable of fighting back; those words made my high school years a misery.

But in the end, that incident with Sharon – that failure to act finally and decisively against her, in defence of myself – was important to my life; it taught me something crucial that I have never forgotten. Through our actions, through our lack of action, we decide our future; we can make ourselves vulnerable or strong, victim or aggressor. And sometimes we have no other choice in life, no other responsibility, other than to act in order to protect ourselves.

EIGHTEEN

I sit on my son's bed. It is a few days since the police have been. The interview turned out to be more of a chat than anything else; the two officers sympathetic to the children, seeming to not want to upset them any more than they already were. I was grateful for their consideration, but still not relaxed. Despite the fact that school resumed that week, I've kept Marty and Beccy home, not wanting them to have to face the questioning of their friends until they're truly ready. I've been discreetly monitoring their behaviour, but other than those first two occasions, we haven't talked directly about the accident.

Martin hasn't invited me into his room like this for a long time. I try to remember the last time he asked me to lie down with him as he dropped off to sleep and can't. I know this is the tragedy of watching my children grow – the tragedy of any mother watching her children grow – the fact that, too late, you miss the things you once found such a chore; the fact that, at some stage, your children stop asking for some things and you can't even remember the last time they wanted it from you.

Marty's eyes, dry and alert now, have that puffy look of many tears shed some time earlier. I stroke his forehead with my hand and trail my fingers through his hair. He used to like to go to sleep like this when he was little; the movement of my hand making his eyes droop and close. Tonight he remains awake, watching me, his mother.

He asked me to come in here with him, but hasn't yet spoken a word.

Now he reaches up and stills my hand, takes it into his own, our fingers interlace. 'I need to talk to you, Mum.'

I lean in low to briefly touch his forehead with my lips. 'I'm always here for you, you know that.'

'I know. That's why I need to tell you something important.'

'Is it about what happened to Chelsea?'

Martin nods.

'I already know what happened,' I whisper. 'There's no need to say anything. I saw it all.'

He looks surprised, but of course I've told no-one that I was standing outside when Chelsea fell, not even my children.

'You saw what happened?' he asks. I nod.

'Did you hear what we were talking about afterwards, what we decided?'

At that I shake my head. 'I didn't hear anything, but I understand what you decided – and why – so you don't have to say anything else at all.'

'But Mum, there's some stuff I need to explain to you. Even though we all promised not to tell.'

I press one finger to his lips. 'Shh,' I say. 'I do understand. There's nothing more to tell me. But it's very, very important that you never discuss this with anybody else. Do you hear me? Do *you* understand? Other people mightn't understand the same way I do. I completely support what you did, but others mightn't . . . they probably won't. But I'm always here for you. I'll always support you. You know that.'

'Okay, Mum, but – '

I sense a movement in the corridor and raise my eyes from Marty's face to see Beccy standing in the doorway with 'Beary', a small brown stuffed bear, held tightly under her arm. Chelsea gave Beary to Beccy soon after she moved in, declaring him too babyish for her, and Beccy has slept with him every night since. 'Mummy, I can't sleep. I asked you to sleep with me. Why are you with Marty when you don't have time to be with *me*?' Beccy's voice, raised and indignant.

I feel the withdrawal beneath my fingertips, the tightening of Marty's skin, the inhalation of his breath. I know he is pulling back, the moment of our privacy is lost; he is unlikely to speak further tonight. But that's okay. Enough has been said. I hold out my free arm to Beccy. She is entitled to my comfort as well. 'Come here, darling. I only sat down with Marty for a little while. Come on and I'll give you a cuddle as well.'

Beccy comes, hugging me hard around my body as she sits on the bed next to me.

I loop one arm around my daughter's shoulders. 'I know both of you are having problems sleeping since what happened to Chelsea. I know she was a good friend to you both. It'll take time for you to get over what happened. I know that. It was terrible what you had to do, what you had to see, but I'll look after you. You don't need to worry about that.'

'She was a nice person, Mummy.' Beccy's face is screwed up with the effort of what she's trying to make me understand.

'I know she was, darling.'

'She let me have all her old dolls, and her old clothes and she shared her make-up with me.' Beccy is crying now, the tears rolling fast down her smooth cheeks.

I hug Beccy closer to me, wiping her tears against my shirt, burying her face where I can't see it. I've never been able to stand seeing my daughter cry like this, true tears that can't be stemmed. It makes me feel inadequate, a mother who cannot properly care for her children, cannot prevent them from being hurt, cannot properly comfort them when they *have* been hurt. It's a great beast, the world: frightening, unpredictable; able to harm one's children in myriad ways. I've always known that: always worried about them at school; on the sports field; at other children's parties. Despite all my concern however, all the effort I've gone to in order to properly prepare my children for whatever they might face in their lives, I had not seen the danger here, pushed up hard against our own back garden. My children had been inadequately safeguarded by a rotting fence that in the end was completely inadequate to contain them.

And now Beccy's tears underline every one of my inadequacies. For someone who has always worked to give her children the perfect childhood, free from concern, these tears do not constitute perfection.

I know Beccy is telling me what she thinks I want to hear: that despite what happened, what has been done, Chelsea was fundamentally a good girl, a good friend. Beccy's always been a careful daughter like this, wanting, perhaps, to protect me, her mother, just as much as I've sought to protect her. She never speaks badly about anyone. It is one of my failings, this pulling of the veil of social niceties so tightly around my children's heads they are unable to speak the truth of how they really feel about people. It is something I wanted so much *not* to do. Beccy can only have got it from me, this desire to welcome everyone as a friend; this inability to speak the truth for fear of hurting someone else; this first step towards welcoming people into your life so that they can hurt you properly.

I pull Beccy fully onto my lap. Her head is nearly level with my own. Even my daughter is growing, up and out of reach. I feel the great tear at my heart that comes at times like this, the realisation that the clock can never be turned back, that time marches relentlessly forward taking my children away from me. Time is not a stream that carries me along evenly with them. Instead, caught in black unseen eddies and unpredictable currents my children will be borne further and further away from me with each day that passes.

'Chelsea was a good person, Mummy. I really loved her.'

'I know darling. I know.'

Beccy lowers her gaze and I place my chin on the top of her head so that her crown of soft hair rests within the curve of my neck. I begin to rock gently. 'I know.'

Out of the corner of my eye I see Marty roll over as if he has had enough of these two females and wants them out of his room. I know that the time for talking to him is past, irretrievable, washed into the middle of the stream and out of sight to somewhere it can never again be caught. Leaning over, I kiss my son's averted cheek. Cradling Beccy hard against me, I carry her back to her bedroom. She sobs against my chest and I wonder if either of my children will ever truly get over this.

NINETEEN

The next day, a Saturday, I look out the window and see what is happening on the other side of the fence. David is cutting down the swing. Setting up a ladder, climbing as high as he is able, he saws at the thick ropes with a knife until they are cut through and the seat falls to the ground, the rope spiralling after it.

I watch as David carefully places the swing seat on the ground and then hits it with an axe, again and again, methodically, almost calmly. From this distance I cannot see the movement of his muscles, the tightness of his torso, the small exhalation of breath as the axe connects. But I can guess at the extreme emotion under which this man is acting. The sympathy I feel for him is almost bottomless.

The swing splinters into smaller and smaller bits. Soon chunks of earth are being cut too, clods of grass flying into the air. Softly, I call Peter over to see. He nods slowly and says, 'I'll go over later. Now isn't the right time.'

David rests for a moment, wiping the sweat from his face with his shirt sleeve. He returns the axe to its proper place in the shed – despite what has happened, he is, after all, a careful man – then he loops together the loose bits of rope and forms the splintered wood of the seat into a small pyramid. Dousing the pile with an accelerant, he steps back and throws a match onto it. There is so little to burn; it takes no time at all to destroy what has been such a source of grief for so many people. The small pyre burns quickly and cleanly, blackening the grass directly beneath. I watch the whole thing, occasionally scanning the inside of the house for movement, but Sandy is nowhere to be seen.

When he has finished, David goes inside. Around half an hour later I hear men talking in my neigh-bours' backyard. Looking outside, I see that they are carrying ropes and spikes and chainsaws. David and

Sandy are having the tree removed. I will be sorry to see it go – it provides good shade in the morning from the hot summer sun – but I know why they do not want that tree there anymore. It is exactly what I would have done as well.

As each branch is lopped and lowered to the ground, two of the men carry it round to the front of the house where I can hear a giant mulching machine at work. The team works smoothly – with few words – almost ritualistically, as the once great tree is slowly and methodically destroyed. It continues all morning. I will not let the children out to watch, so from time to time they peek from the bathroom window. For the whole period David sits on his back deck and watches. When the branch that the swing was hanging from is felled, he turns away and covers his eyes.

Towards lunchtime, when there is only the bare trunk of the tree to be cut, Peter decides it's time to go over. Removing a six-pack of beer from the fridge he walks down the street and around the corner, to the other man's house. I see him appear on the back deck. Each clutching a drink, the two men sit together while the trunk is cut to the ground and a stump grinder is brought in to remove the remainder. They sit together for the rest of the afternoon. At one stage they share a pizza, but at no time do I see Sandy.

TWENTY

There is very little Peter and I have fought over during our marriage, but when he closes the door to our bedroom I can sense he isn't happy. I'd heard the garage door closing about ten minutes earlier, so knew he'd been able to make it home. He was meant to be at a meeting that afternoon, one with international clients that had been planned for months.

Peter moves to the bed, sits on the edge and looks over to where I stand in front of the mirror putting on my jewellery.

I speak first, 'You made it.'

'I had to come. I wanted to be there, for Dave.'

I nod. I understand how he feels.

'I've spoken to the kids,' he continues.

'Yes?'

'They've told me you won't let them go to the funeral. Clair, I really believe they should be allowed to come if they want to.'

I shake my head. 'No Peter, I don't agree. Tiffany will be over soon; I've asked her to keep an eye on the kids while we're away. I don't want them coming. I don't want them to be subjected to any more than they've already experienced.'

I've already had this conversation with Martin and don't feel I have the energy to do it again. Martin was very angry with me when I told him that he and Beccy were staying at home. 'But Mum,' he said, 'how else are we supposed to say goodbye to her? It's not fair. I really want to go to the funeral.' It was one of Marty's strengths – when he really wanted something he would put a lot of effort into getting it. He wasn't like Beccy, wanting so many things every day and often wearing me down to get them. Marty was solid, stolid. I knew that he'd thought things through; that going to the funeral was truly what he desired.

And what he said had resonated with me. I remember wanting some things so badly as a child and being thwarted by my mother's seeming indifference to my deeply held desires. But I know that being a good mother means there are times when I must do things that make my children dislike me. There's no cure for that. The burden of responsibility lies with me. It has always lain with me, from that very first day when Peter walked out of the house back to work, and left me sitting on the couch with a scrawny, scrawling month-old baby who I knew would need all of my protection for the rest of my life. Nobody had ever said that it would be easy. It hadn't been easy telling Martin that he and Beccy weren't going to Chelsea's funeral. And it seems as if Peter is about to make it less so.

'But that's ridiculous, Clair!' he says. 'Of course they need to come to the funeral.'

I hold my hands steady, trying to find the back of an earring so that I can fix it into my lobe. The quiver that's begun in my hands makes it difficult. The truth is that I knew Peter wouldn't be happy with my decision to leave the kids at home, which is precisely why I didn't discuss it with him earlier. In fact, I'd secretly hoped he wouldn't be able to get out of his meeting.

'I don't think so, Peter. I think letting them go would be the wrong thing to do.'

'Clair, we have to let them go. It's a way of saying goodbye. I have to say I completely support them on this. I think they've even written something to say. I know they've got some things they want to bring with them.'

Something to bring with them, something to say ... My eyes are still on the mirror in front of me, but I realise that, with my hands shaking as they are, there's no way I'm going to be able to get the back of my earring to connect with the front. I pull it from my ear and remove the other one as well, letting them fall into my jewellery case. They're ruby drops, a wedding present from Peter, too dressy to wear often.

'Well Peter ...' I take a deep breath and turn to look at him. I know that in many ways Marty is just like his dad. Peter is obviously determined that the kids will come today, so I'm ready to do a deal. I don't have much choice. 'Look, I'll agree to the kids coming,' I say, 'just so long as you agree to them sitting with us where we can keep a good eye on how they're going. And under no circumstances are they to be allowed to participate in the service. Will you at least support me on that?'

Peter reaches out his hands and takes mine. 'All right, let's agree to that then,' he says.

Marty and Beccy sit to Peter's right, next to Tabby and Sam, while Mel and Joe make up the end of the pew. My children have chosen their own clothes for the funeral. Martin has on a long-sleeved grey shirt with dark jeans and Beccy wears one of the tops which Chelsea had passed on to her the day before the accident. The top is too big, but Beccy has put on a tight T-shirt underneath and somehow the combination is just right – sombre, respectful. It matches her face.

I've never been to this church before and everything seems so dark; the stained-glass windows let in very little light and the minister is dressed in heavy black robes. The red roses decorating the altar and the top of the white casket do nothing to alleviate the gloom, seeming, if possible, to heighten it.

The minister gives an introduction to Chelsea – who she was, her life – but I know, and I'm sure Sandy is painfully aware, that while his intoned words are designed to not cause pain, neither do they provide much comfort. There is no doubt this older man is completely out of his depth celebrating the life of someone so young; his use of standard phrases revealing that he never met Chelsea, has no knowledge of the cut and thrust of her young life.

A friend of David and Sandy's speaks after the minister – someone from their old life, I imagine, as I've never seen him before – reading carefully prepared words of his own and then a heartwrenching speech on behalf of both Sandy and David who, I see, have their heads tucked in together. Obviously they feel unable to stand in front of us all and bare their grief; I can't say I blame them.

Chelsea's teacher from last year speaks next; she is a younger woman and she cries as she talks, wiping her tears from her nose and the paper from which she reads. It is a beautiful and correct speech. This time the flavour is right – the connection made with Chelsea's youth by someone who knew her well – but still somehow it is as if the girl she speaks about could be any one of her adored students; an idealised paper cut-out. Does it always come to this in the end, I wonder? The ridges of a human life being smoothed out in the final celebration, with people so careful about what they say and do that there is little room for the individual personality to be revealed.

I sense movement to my right and turn to see Marty, Beccy, Tabby and Sam rising to their feet. They have pieces of paper clutched in their hands and Marty carries a small bag. They begin to move past Peter and me, towards the centre aisle. Holding up my arm, I block them. 'What are they doing?' I whisper to Peter.

'I don't know.'

We both look up at the children. 'We're going to read something and do something special for Chelsea,' says Martin. 'It's already been arranged.'

I grip Peter's arm with my free hand. 'You promised me . . .'

'I know,' he replies. 'I told them no . . .'

I look at Martin. His head is tilted to one side and his eyes are bright. He knows he is defying me. I remember how he wanted to talk to me that night in his bedroom. I have no idea what he wants to say today. There's no way he's going up there to speak.

By now people are turning around to look at us. Mel has a frown on her face.

'Peter, do something!' My hand has begun to shake again.

Peter looks at my hand and then at me. 'Sit down, Martin,' he says.

'But Dad . . .'

'Sit down, Martin. Sit down, Beccy. Tabitha and Sam, you can go through if you want to.'

Confused, Tabby and Sam look at Marty. He shakes his head and together the four of them sit down again.

I face the front of the church and see Sandy looking at me. She has an unreadable expression on her face. As people rustle and resettle, readying themselves for the ceremony to continue, Sandy, once again, turns towards the front of the church.

Chelsea's schoolmates form a guard of honour as the casket is carried from the church, the petals of the roses moving slightly in the breeze which begins as the congregation exits. There are tears and tissues, the gloom of the day settling downwards like a huge lid.

Towards the end, after the coffin has been loaded into the back of the hearse, Sandy comes up to me. I didn't step forward earlier when she was mingling with the other mourners; I've expressed my sympathy so often to her that I really didn't know what else to say and I'm embarrassed over what happened in the church.

I point now to where Chelsea's classmates stand. 'It's wonderful that the school has supported Chelsea, and you, the way they have.'

Sandy nods. 'Yes.' She sighs. 'But she wasn't really good friends with any of them. The truth is she'll be forgotten, the ranks will close again and it'll be as if she was never at school with them at all. I doubt many of them will even remember her in a few years' time.'

Sandy reaches out and takes one of my hands in hers. 'She was finding it hard to make friends, you know that, don't you, Clair? I know she didn't come across this way, and she never liked me to talk about it, but she was shy, very shy. She felt comfortable with your children, Clair; she truly loved them. I wish you'd let them speak today, to do what they felt they needed to.' Sandy drops her head and begins to cry, alone in her grief, always alone, no matter how many people might surround her.

Reaching out, I hug her to me and for one moment, one giddy, unsettling moment, I feel sorry that I stopped the children from reading – anything to help water down this woman's grief – but still I know it is more important that I keep my children safe than that I regard the sensibilities of this woman, no matter how deep her sorrow or how pressing her need.

TWENTY-ONE

We are home from the wake. Peter has hurried back to work and Marty has invited Tabby and Sam over. I am fine with that. It will distract them from being angry with me.

I've changed out of my funeral clothes and as I walk out onto the back deck to see what the children are doing, the gloom of the afternoon disappears for a moment; the sun comes out from behind the clouds where it has been shrouded all day and I see the children, bathed in full sunlight, standing on the other side of the fence – Chelsea's side – in the hollow where the tree used to be, near where the underground creek flows. They are standing in a circle around a large metal biscuit tin. I recognise the tin; it has been taken from the back of one of my kitchen cupboards where it has been stored for many years, almost forgotten. There is no way I can hear what the children are saying, but I know that if I move any closer, they're likely to see me, so I stay where I am and watch.

Marty points to Beccy and she moves a little further into the circle. She lowers her head and reads from a piece of paper in her hands. She has her back to me and her brown hair is multi-toned in the sunlight, shot through with gold flecks from the summer sun. She has something under her arm, but I can't see what it is. When she has finished speaking she folds her paper in half and places it inside the biscuit tin, then removes the object from under her arm and holds it for a moment against her face, giving it a kiss. I can see now that it is Beary, the beloved stuffed toy given to her by Chelsea. Leaning over, Beccy places Beary inside the biscuit tin as well.

Marty points at Sammy next. He has one hand tightly closed and holds his slip of paper in the other hand, but he doesn't read from it, staring instead into space as he speaks. He is profiled in the sunlight and I realise just how much like Mel he looks – same nose, same chin, same open face. When Sammy has finished, he opens his fist and the sun hits the faceted crystal quartz that sits on his palm, throwing small rainbows over all of the children. Sam is an avid rock collector and I know this crystal is one of his favourites. I remember his father buying it for him and how excited Sammy had been. Then he too leans over and places his note and the crystal in the tin.

Now Tabitha moves forward slightly. She is gripping her note tightly, trying hard to stop her hand from trembling. She is still dressed in the rainbow of colour that she wore to the funeral: favourite red shoes, blue pants, yellow top and, slung over her shoulder, an emerald-green shirt, brilliant in the sunlight. I recognise it as a new one she has only worn once or twice. I thought how well it matched the red tint of her hair when I first saw her in it. I also remember Chelsea admiring it and Sandy offering to get her one just like it the next time they went shopping. I think now how well it would also have matched Chelsea's blonde hair. When Tabitha has finished speaking she removes the shirt from her shoulder, folds it carefully and places it, and her note, in the tin.

Marty's turn. His note is folded tightly and he doesn't bother to open it as he speaks. He doesn't talk for long, his head bowed the entire time. When he's finished he reaches into his pocket and takes out a small red velvet box I've never seen before. Leaning over he places the box and note into the tin. As he straightens up, he wipes his nose and eyes, I can imagine that his face is stained with tears.

Together, all four children bend down and each take a corner of the tin, carrying it over to where a hole has been dug within the loose soil where the old tree once stood. There they bury the tin, covering it carefully.

I have watched the children stupidly, without moving, spellbound by the solemnity of this almost pagan ritual of grief and love. My emotions, scrunched like a ball at the base of my throat, have made even breathing difficult. And then, as the children finish burying the biscuit tin, it is fear which takes the uppermost hand. I stopped the children from reading those notes at the funeral today, but still I don't know what they contain. Perhaps it is the truth about what happened the day Chelsea died; perhaps it is sorrow, couched in terms damning enough to implicate my children. I cannot know, and now those words have been placed in a biscuit tin and buried in Chelsea's own backyard.

Time is of the essence. Even now, for all I know, Mel might also be looking at the scene from one of her back rooms, listening from the bathroom window. I know that my actions must not be too extreme, too agitated and that I must be careful of what I say in front of Mel's children, for there is no knowing what they will carry back to her, even if not deliberately. I know that parents are capable of imputing thoughts and creating stories from even the most innocent of their children's words and gestures.

And then of course there is Sandy, and David. They had been saying goodbye to the last of the people at the wake when Peter, Mel, Joe and I had said our own goodbyes. How would Sandy feel to come home and see these children in her backyard, standing in the damp, friable ground where the tree and swing that had killed her daughter had once stood?

I decide to go with my best bet – Beccy. Martin has been too recalcitrant lately to be the initial choice.

'Beccy,' I call, low and controlled, the voice I might use with an overwrought horse, or a kitten I am trying to entice into my home. All the children's heads snap around, all four looking in my direction, their emotions difficult to read. 'Beccy, can you come over here please? Now?' The last word with a dangerous wobble that threatens to throw off balance the calm of the rest of the sentence, like a freight train hurtling round a dangerous bend, its last carriage suddenly, inexplicably airborne.

The children move towards me in a huddle, unwilling, it seems, to allow only one of their number to face me – and whatever is coming – alone. It is a dangerous loyalty, I know that, a loyalty which could see all of them blamed for the transgressions of only one. Children are unpredictable like this: at times willing to throw one of their own forward for sacrifice; at others closing rank with fierce tribal instinct. And these contradictory impulses seem to occur at random, so that it is only via memory, only by dredging up thoughts of their own childhoods, that adults have any idea of motivation, any hope of understanding these strange beings who have been created from us, but who stand alone, independent, believing they are completely capable of making their own decisions, forging their own paths.

Each in turn, the children bob under the fence, then, together, they make their way over to me.

'What were you children doing over there? Don't you know how Sandy would feel if she saw you? What were you burying?' I am barely capable of making myself wait until they stand before me.

Martin, the self-appointed spokesperson, steps forward. 'It was some things that we were leaving for Chelsea. Some things you wouldn't let us leave for her at the church. We had to find some way to do it properly.'

'For Chelsea? What types of things?'

'Things that she might like.'

Now Tabby steps forward to join him. 'They were things we thought she should have. Things she liked when she was alive.'

And Beccy. 'And Mummy, we had to do *something*.'

'What about the notes; what did they say?' I will not, cannot, reveal to them how much I want the answer to that question.

'Just our thoughts,' Sammy replies, his voice carrying, pure and clear. Sammy – the most silent of them all. The fact he is speaking now, like this, gives the event more importance. If I had been smarter, Sammy is the one I would have pressed first.

'What types of thoughts?' I hope that the steel in my voice will be enough for them to tell me more.

'They were just private thoughts, Mum. Us telling Chelsea how we felt about her. You wouldn't understand.' Martin shakes his head, obviously so sure that I would not.

'Well, I think you should go and unbury that tin and bring it over here now.'

There is silence, a stubborn silence, a silence so deep and so unified from children not used to, or comfortable with, silence, that I know my request has been refused, completely and finally.

I try a different tack. 'What will I tell Chelsea's mum when she realises something's been buried in her backyard? It could upset her badly to know what you've done.'

'Don't worry, we'll tell her. We'll explain to her.' Martin again.

'No you will not. You will remove it!' I'm angry and the tone of my voice reveals it.

Again silence, the sound of my words dying away, the crying of a bird in the distance, the stubborn hum of defiant children. And then there is movement in the house I am facing and I see Sandy, standing on her back deck, still in the shadow. She is hard to make out, but I know that the children and I can be seen clearly, in the full sun. I raise a hand to her and the children turn to see who I'm waving at. And slowly, very slowly, I see the other woman's hand rise – just a little – in greeting, before she turns, back to the deep, dark stillness of the house.

So I know that it's too late. Whatever is contained in those notes in the tin will stay there and frankly that worries me; in fact, it terrifies me.

TWENTY-TWO

*N*ow is not the time for letting go. The children, Marty in particular, are testing their limits in a way they never have before. It happens, when children press against the safety constraints you have set for them. There are always judgements to be made. Which friends can they invite home, go to visit? Can they take the bus, walk home from school? I remember once, in early high school, being asked to draw the limits of where we could go by ourselves at different ages: within the house when we were two; the yard as children; down the street; into town. Each child in the class had differing limits at varying ages. I think now that what the teacher had been trying to show us was that the wider you are allowed to roam, the greater the level of trust you have been given and therefore the greater your responsibilities. The corollary, of course, is that if you cannot prove your trustworthiness, you cannot expect additional freedom.

I will not punish my children for pushing against the limits I have set for them, but based on their response, based on what we are facing, I know that what I must do is reset the limits, which once were sufficient. I will monitor much more carefully where they go and what they do. I have no choice.

The day after the funeral, I open the phonebook and find a handyman to fix the rotting fence – back and sides. I will begin by reinforcing my children's physical boundaries, shoring up my control. I know it won't be that easy in all aspects of our lives, but I will try.

TWENTY-THREE

I answer the knock on the door even though I don't want to. Peter has arranged this, a counsellor to see the children. He has held back for a time, but obviously now feels he can do so no longer, initiating this visit as his way of dealing with things, so different to my own. He is a practical man, my husband, believes that everything can be fixed with money and application, the right shoulder pushed against the right door at the right time. He believes in calling people in, the legacy of his years at work spent as a manager: delegate, spread responsibility, share duties. I, however, am different. I know that many points stop with me.

We had talked about this a few nights earlier when he'd come home. It was late, and I was already in bed, but still he was determined to talk, his hand upon my shoulder, shaking me awake.

'I just need to know the kids are okay, Clair.'

I turned over in bed to look at him, knowing he would not be ignored. 'Of course they're okay,' I replied. 'I'm looking after them.'

Peter sighed. He'd pulled the chair I usually place my half-dirty clothes on hard up to my side of the bed. In the moonlight I could see, in a heap in the corner of the room, the previously carefully laid out clothes that I had planned on re-wearing for my walk the next morning. Peter raised his right hand and smoothed it over his hair. It's a gesture he uses when he's feeling vulnerable or helpless: the day he asked me to marry him; as he crouched beside me as I was curled over with the pain of childbirth; that night. 'I'm really concerned about what the kids might be feeling after what happened. They're just seeming so, oh I don't know, contained or something, depressed maybe.'

I sat up slightly, paused, choosing my words carefully. 'Well, that's right I guess. They're feeling scared and vulnerable. No-one knows our children as well as we do. We need to look after them. They need protecting now, defending from all sorts of people.'

Peter sighed, 'Of course they need looking after, Clair. That's our job as parents and we've – well, you in particular – you've always done it well. But maybe what they need protecting from now are the terrors of their own minds. What they saw was horrible. It could so easily have happened to either of them instead of Chelsea. They must have all sorts of questions, questions about mortality most of us don't have to face till we're much older. Questions we really need to understand and address. I think that's something beyond us. I really think we need to call in a professional for this.'

I shook my head, annoyed by his statements, his intrusion. Even though he hadn't seen what I'd seen, surely he could trust me on this. 'I don't think what happened to Chelsea has affected them in the way you seem to think. I really don't think they've got any fear that what happened to her might have happened to them. Don't you see, Peter? What Marty and Beccy need now is to know we support them and love them. We need to keep them safe from the outside world, not welcome it in.'

My irritation must have been reflected in my tone because Peter responded in kind then, his voice low and angry as he stood up to leave the room.

'Despite what you might think, Clair, despite what you believe, there are times when even you can't do absolutely everything.'

So when Peter informed me this morning that he'd already arranged this counsellor, I knew I couldn't refuse. Not because a counsellor would help, but because if I didn't agree to it, Peter would push until he got his way. He doesn't usually exert pressure on me at home, that's something he saves for work, but once he's decided to do something here, it's not possible to completely thwart him.

She – the counsellor, Pat – asks to see the children together and I take them into the lounge room. I tell Pat that I'll sit in with them, that they're too young to talk to a stranger about this by themselves. Whether she's happy with this arrangement or not, she murmurs her approval; she sits down, arranging everyone so that she's facing the children with me to one side of her, also facing them.

Pat is middle-aged, hair firmly styled, wearing a modern version of a twin-set and pearls. She projects calm and certainty and, if all else fails, she seems quite capable of taking my children and comforting them against her chest. She is the full package, so much the caricature of what a counsellor should be that it's hard for me not to smile.

But I can't afford to underestimate anyone and I hate the fact that this woman is inside my house. I'm angry both with Peter and the chain of events – beginning all those months ago when Chelsea first moved into the house behind ours – that's led to this. My children are apprehensive. Marty has begun to bite his fingernails and, with no fingernails left, he's taken to tearing at the skin of his nail bed. Even from where I'm sitting I can see the ragged raw edges of his cuticles. I long to take his hands inside mine to soothe his burning fingers with my touch; I want to fold him into my heart; to take his hurt into my body; to stand in place of him so that he need not hurt as he does – but of course none of this is possible. Despite all my efforts, my role as shield for my children against the world has gradually broken down as they've grown and started to assume responsibility for their own behaviour. Now I can see that Marty has moved beyond even that; he is assuming responsibility for his little sister.

He sits slightly angled, facing the counsellor, so that his body is just in front of Beccy's. She, in turn, is pressed hard into the space behind his body and the back of the couch, her eyes peering over the top of her brother's shoulder.

Pat addresses them together, leaning forward slightly, her hands resting lightly against her thighs. 'Now, Martin and Rebecca, your parents have asked me here today because they're concerned for you. Do you know why that is?'

When the response from the children is deafening silence, she tries again. 'What about you, Martin? Do you have any idea why your parents might be concerned for you?'

I try to give him a reassuring smile: *Don't worry, darling, you don't have to say anything at all if you don't want to.* I wish I'd said this to Marty before this woman came into our lives; I've not prepared very well – after all, this is a new experience for me too. But Marty is not looking at me, his eyes are firmly on Pat. 'It's because of what happened to Chelsea, isn't it?'

Pat nods. 'Yes, it is. How do you feel about what happened?'

Marty's face is screwed up. 'What do you mean?'

'Well, when something like that happens, it can be difficult for anyone who was there, particularly for someone who was a friend.'

Marty nods. 'Yes, we were all sad. Very sad. We liked Chelsea a lot.'

Behind Marty, Beccy is nodding vigorously. 'We liked to play with her and she gave me her old clothes. She had lots of good games and the best bedroom!' Her eyes are open wide as they are when she's excited. Eyes so vividly blue that when she focuses on you it's like being caught in a beam of light. I can see that Pat is smiling at her; Beccy is an easy child for adults to warm to. Marty can be a little harder, and it's him I worry about in this situation more than Beccy. Particularly because I know how protective of Beccy he's been lately.

Pat looks over Marty's shoulder to Beccy. 'When you think of Chelsea, how do you feel, Rebecca?'

'I miss her and I miss the swing. We used to have fun on that. I miss going to visit her house and having her come over here.'

'Did you play together a lot?'

Beccy is nodding, 'Yes a lot.'

'What kind of games did you play together?'

'Fun games!' Beccy beams.

'We used to play all sorts of games,' Marty explains. 'Us and the other neighbours, Sammy and Tabby. We played together all the time.'

'Rebecca, you mentioned the swing earlier. Did you play on it a lot?'

'Yeah.' She looks over at me. 'But Mummy didn't like me to go on the swing. She worried when I went too high.'

'But you had fun on the swing, did you?'

Beccy nods.

'Have you been on the swing since what happened to Chelsea?'

Both children shake their heads, but it's Marty who answers. 'Her father cut it down after it happened.'

This doesn't seem to surprise Pat. 'I guess that was one way for him to cope with what happened.'

Suddenly Marty blurts out. 'We had a special ceremony, you know. We said goodbye to Chelsea in the backyard. We all gave her some things we knew she'd like.'

Pat is nodding. 'Did you? That was very sensible of you. It's important to say goodbye properly. Was that your mum's idea?'

Both the kids shake their heads. 'No,' Marty says, 'it was ours.'

Beccy looks over at me again. 'Mummy was a bit cross with us.' Gently I move my head back and forwards, warning her to stop. I hope Pat doesn't turn to look at me.

'Well,' she says, 'sometimes even mummies become upset by things. But if that was what you felt you needed to do, then it was probably the right thing for you. How did you feel after that special ceremony?'

Both the children echo, 'Good.' But then Beccy adds, 'I miss Beary, that's what I put in the box for Chelsea. But I know how much she loved him before she gave him to me, so that's okay.'

'And what about you, Martin? Did you put something in the box for Chelsea?'

Martin looks at me. I see wariness in his eyes, but I realise it's not Pat he's worried about, it's me. 'I bought something for her, with all my saved pocket-money.' I know that Martin has been saving for an expensive new computer game; the amount he'd already put aside was substantial.

'What was that, Martin?' Pat's voice is warm, inviting. 'Do you want to tell me?'

He lowers his head, unable to look at me. 'I bought her a gold ring, with a green stone. She liked green.'

Pat nods. 'Chelsea was very important to you, wasn't she, Martin?'

Again Martin looks at me and I know this is a moment of tested loyalties. If he admits how he felt about Chelsea, will that be betraying me? The truth is, I knew it would come to this one day, Marty's feelings moving from me to another, but I hadn't expected it now, like this.

Finally my son speaks. 'I loved Chelsea. Even with everything she did that was wrong, I loved her.'

And now I know for sure. It has been confirmed by Martin's actions as well as his words – the use of his precious, carefully hoarded money for a ring that would never be seen, or worn, by its intended recipient – that girl, that girl next door with the blonde hair and knowing face came into our lives and took my son away from me. Martin's initial infatuation might have been normal enough, and in the usual course of events he would have grown up and away from her, forming other friendships, pursuing other relationships. But now that Chelsea is dead she is forever captured in a time and space where she is young and beautiful and where Marty finds her irresistible, despite, or perhaps even because of, what he had to do in order to care for his sister. For him, Chelsea has become immortalised – a tragic, beautiful, doomed creature, never to be forgotten.

It is more than I can stand, the confirmation that that girl possesses such a space in my son's life. I feel my breathing grow shallower, sense the greyness behind my eyes. Excusing myself I move into the kitchen. Leaning over the sink I breathe deeply until I feel control returning, until I can once again face Pat and the children. When, finally, I re-enter the lounge room, I catch the tail end of what Martin is saying. 'I kind of understand, and it's okay for the moment. I'm managing.' *Managing what*, I wonder, but I know it's not the time to ask.

Pat is looking me directly in the eye. She is standing at the door about to leave and I can feel my body almost relaxing when she places a hand on one of mine and speaks. 'Well Clair, I'm very pleased to say that both children seem to be doing fine . . . but maybe we need to make a time for you? I sense some understandable anxiety in you about what's happened, and there's the risk it might rub off onto the children. What do you think about making a time with me or one of my colleagues? Soon, sometime soon. Don't leave it too long.'

TWENTY-FOUR

lthough I would never admit it to her, Pat is right, there *is* an uneasy tilt to the universe for me these days. I've tried to be so strong for my children. To deal with problems before they've arisen, to stay calm in the face of what threatens us. Until recently, I've felt successful, but the combination of the children's backyard ceremony and the intrusion of Pat into our lives at Peter's insistence – against my wishes, when he has always been so supportive of my parenting decisions – has unsettled me and I can feel it: the apprehension that lies at my core, mostly still and hidden, but always there, always waiting to claim me.

There is a sense of fragility about my life now. The certainties upon which my mothering has been based

– the idea that children can be kept safe within the confines of a home, for example – have been eroded. I know now that people can come into your world and change the course of your children's lives without you even being aware of what is happening.

The sense that my mothering has been ineffective seems to be dissolving the underpinnings of my existence. The simple pleasures, which once would have eased me through the day – the children coming home from school; relaxing in bed with a good book; lying with my head on Peter's lap watching a movie; the enjoyment of good food; even the feel of my own body warm and pliant beneath my hands in the shower – none of these things are capable of bringing me joy; they do not provide the solidity, the tethering, I suddenly need. It's as if I'm ephemeral, no longer possessing any substance, and an inquiring finger daring to touch my body would find itself sinking into a deep, black nothingness. The truth is that we all acknowledge the fragility of the body – cut it and it bleeds, squeeze too hard and it bruises – but the invisible injuries to the mind are not so obvious. There are so many mysteries of consciousness, so many chinks that we can fall into when negotiating our way through existence.

I've had these feelings of uncertainty before, although never on this scale. Like many of the rhythms of my life, a woman's life, I've always regarded them as transient, convincing myself that if I don't acknowledge them, one day they'll simply leave and I'll be fit and whole again; if I pretended everything was all right, it would be. I've often wondered how many other people are the same – the plastered smile, the nodded hello, the pretence that everything is tolerable, so that in time it would be.

But now it is wearing me down – the lack of sleep; the sensation that my emotions are seeping out of my increasingly porous body. At night, I huddle against Peter's back, my legs curled under me, not cold, but seeking the substance I suddenly lack. As if wrapping myself into a ball against the rock of his body might draw me back from where I am. But even that is not enough; the vast empty-coldness of the night is not to be denied. I have tried facing it in different ways, none of them entirely successful. Alternately I lie in bed, eyes open or closed, away from my husband or pressed against him; I rise and read; pace the corridor; surf the internet; take increasingly earlier morning walks.

If Peter has noticed my nocturnal restlessness, he doesn't say, and, given that he's such a heavy sleeper, it's possible that he does not. I'd like to tell him what's happening to me – his assurance, his calm, his male solidity could probably help me now – but I can't tell him how I feel without telling him why. And since I can't do that, I must deal with this alone.

The problem is that my worry is reducing me to its level, tightening around me like a straitjacket, making it impossible for me to see beyond the small boundaries of my fear, making it impossible to achieve more than a fraction of my potential. And in order to continue to shield my children, I will need to harness every ounce of my power.

TWENTY-FIVE

The letter in my letterbox has no stamp, so I know someone has dropped it in personally. Curious, I open it immediately, standing in the driveway, the sun on my back.

What has happened is unbearable. I have made her bed, washed the last of her dirty clothes, hung up the clean dresses in her cupboard. I pretend that she is away: a school camp; with her grandparents. I imagine she will come back to claim these clothes and be annoyed that her room isn't exactly as she left it.

If I think about the reality it is unbearable.

I'm reading a lot, anything I can get my hands on. I lose myself in books, because if I think of the reality of her I cannot breathe, my head will not lift itself. I can eat only by imagining her walking through that door. It would be so easy for me to end my suffering by never eating again, a long drawn-out tribute to my daughter, to my grief. And I would be helping no-one in the process.

People don't understand the depth of my grief. They think that because I don't sob uncontrollably in their presence that I'm all right. But they can't know, they can't understand that I don't do this because I can't face what would otherwise claim me. An emptiness stretching to infinity, a despair that I'm here and she is gone, the unbearability of what I'll wake up to day after day – the fact of her empty bed, her clothes hanging waiting in the wardrobe. These things are so terrible they cannot be faced without a buffer of denial.

I fear that a glimpse of my true suffering would blight your soul forever. But Clair, dear Clair, it's time that I rejoined the world. I would love it if you would come over and see me some time soon. I will be home. I never go anywhere anymore.

Sandy

I sit now, in her kitchen. The sun slanting through the window as it has all the other times I've been here, as if it has no knowledge that the lives of the two women on which it beams have been changed irrevocably. The granite benchtops no longer glitter. They have been laid over with a black cloth. Like a Victorian woman Sandy has shrouded the things which once brought her such happiness. I understand this, applaud it almost. In the midst of so much *not* being right, this one thing at least is the right thing to do.

When Sandy has finished making coffee, she sits at the table and cries, salty drops into her cup. I think of the tears of a giant Alice in Wonderland, drowning any creature that stands beneath her. Like Alice, Sandy has grown bigger in her grief, squeezing into oblivion the needs of anyone who stands beside her. None can compare their emotions with a woman who has lost her only child. I cannot, in any case, share with her my fears for my own children.

'Thanks for coming over,' she manages to get out. 'I know it's hard for people to visit me. They don't know what to say. I understand that. Hell,' she almost laughs, '*I* wouldn't know what to say to me.' She rubs her eyes with a tissue from the box that has not left her side the whole time I have been here. Scattered around the room are similar boxes, as if she is afraid to be too far away from them. 'I'm crying less now, you know. The first couple of weeks, David would come home with a couple of tissue boxes a day. I wore all the skin away from under my nose. He said he envied me, able to grieve for as long as I want while he's expected to go back to work, put a brave face on things.' She reaches out her hand and grasps one of mine, 'But the truth is, Clair, for the first time since I had Chelsea, I wish I had a job to go to, something to fill my days, something to keep my mind off how much I'm missing her. So I've decided to do some volunteer work at the homeless shelter. I'm going down there tomorrow to see how best I can be put to use.' She pushes a plastic bag across the table towards me. 'And I've started trying to sort through some of Chelsea's things. I want you to have this.'

I pick up the bag and open it. Nestled within, smelling of fresh laundering and expectation and the promise of growth and life, is a high school uniform – the uniform Chelsea would have worn to her new school, Marty's school, this year.

'It's never been worn. I thought you could use it, for Beccy. I bought it for Chelsea as soon as we heard she'd been accepted into the school. I was going to buy her another one just before she started. In case she grew.' Sandy shrugs. 'You know how it is, they grow like weeds at this age.'

I try to push the bag back to her. 'I can't,' I say. 'I can't take this.'

She rests her hand against mine, firmly. 'I insist, Clair. I don't have any use for it now. Chelsea never wore it. It's the first thing of hers I've given away. It's the right thing to do, for me. Please will you take it? You were so good helping me get her into the school and the uniforms are so expensive. Better you have it than someone else, or that it sits unused in her cupboard.'

'Oh God, Sandy.' I hardly know what to say. The last thing I want is this uniform that belonged to Chelsea, but Sandy's made it clear there can be no refusal. 'It's just so terrible what happened,' I finally murmur; inadequate words, useless words. 'Such a dreadful accident and something that could have happened to any one of the children.'

'Oh yes, Clair. That's one of the things that keeps me awake at night. What if it had been one of your kids, or Mel's? It's horrible for me that it was Chelsea, of course. But I don't know how I could've lived with myself if it was one of your kids who hurt themselves on *our* swing. That fucking, fucking swing.' Sandy's hands are clenched, her knuckles white. 'If only I'd been firmer with her about that. Not allowed her to swing so high. That was my big failing, Clair.' The tears are falling again. 'I could never discipline her properly. I loved her too much. Now I see what a huge mistake that was.' She shakes her head. 'I just keep wondering how it happened. How such a simple, stupid accident happened. David won't even let me talk about it. Every time I bring it up, it's as though I'm trying to blame him, when all I'm doing is trying to understand.'

She catches my eyes, impossible for me to turn from her gaze.

'The children told me what they did, you know?' Her eyes are huge, magnified by her tears. 'It was so lovely of them. They came over last week, specially to tell me about the tin, in case I found it one day and wondered what it was. I couldn't believe it when I opened the door and saw the four of them there. I hadn't seen them all together like that, you know, since the day it happened. And they just seemed, oh I don't know, bright and solid standing there, and they reminded me of Chelsea. But not in a bad way, Clair.'

Hearing my name recalls me to where I am, to what Sandy's saying. For when I heard that my children had visited her the week before, without me, without me even knowing, I felt the coldness within my chest, the erratic beat in my heart. I try to concentrate on what Sandy is saying. But my mind is on other things – what other barriers have my children pushed through lately without my knowledge?

Sandy seems oblivious to my agitation. 'It was so overwhelming to see them all there like that. But they made me remember that Chelsea once existed exactly as they did, not just inside a grieving mother's mind. I wanted to hug them all to me so I could remember what it feels like to have a child's arms wrapped around my neck.' She laughs. 'But I didn't want to scare them, so I acted as serious as they were.' Her voice becomes deep now, taking on the formal tone she'd used to welcome my children into her home. 'I invited them in and asked if they wanted something to eat or drink, but they very politely declined and then they told me what they'd done. How they'd each written something to Chelsea and selected something of theirs that she'd loved; special things, you know, things that were difficult for them to part with, and that they'd buried them in the garden where they used to play. I was touched, Clair, so touched.'

I'm unable to reply, but it doesn't seem to worry Sandy. She's obviously planned to tell me this, all of it, and is not to be stopped. She shakes her head. 'They were nervous, you know. I think it was terribly hard for them being here. But they were so thoughtful. They told me you thought I might be upset or sad if I found the tin, but Clair, how could I ever, ever be upset with your children, or Mel's? They were Chelsea's friends. They brought her so much joy when she was alive.' Sandy is crying again, the tissues balled in her hand a soggy mass.

I reach over and put my arm around her, patting her on the shoulder. I feel as if I am pushing through a solid mass; I have to force myself to touch her. There is no way I feel up to consoling this woman, but she must not have any inkling of what I'm truly feeling – the horror, the fear.

Sandy turns and hugs me and now it's my turn to feel the press of her wet face against my chest. I remember that day, surely not as long ago as it seems, when she first hugged me and I'd believed myself truly understood for the first time in my life. I'd felt she and I were forming a friendship that would endure forever.

Sandy pulls away; there's more she wants to say. 'But I was sad as well because they'd come through the front door. When Chelsea was alive they used to come over so casually, under the fence. And even though I didn't want to scare them, I began to cry . . . really cry! I couldn't help myself. Because you know what those four children had done?' Looking up at me, Sandy demands a response. I shake my head, it's all I can manage, and she continues. 'They'd given me the greatest gift a mother could have. After what they told me I knew that it wasn't just in my heart that Chelsea would live forever, but that she'd also live in the hearts of your and Mel's children. In the end they all hugged me and that was the most comforted I've felt since Chelsea died.'

I listen to all of this – this confession; this sorrow; the actions of the children – but the emotions Sandy's story evoke in me are not what they should be. I know I should be feeling sympathy for Sandy and pride that my children have tried to comfort her. But instead what I feel is only fear, pushing away all before it. Fear that my control over Marty and Beccy is eroding faster than I'd realised. How can I protect them if I don't know what they're doing? What they're saying? Where they are? I feel heat build in the back of my neck and pulse through my body.

'I just wanted you to know this, Clair,' Sandy is continuing, still unaware of my distress. 'I wanted you to know how much they all loved Chelsea. The children were devastated by what happened. I think it'll take a long time for them to recover.' She sits up straight now as if about to reveal what she's really invited me here to tell me. 'There's something else I've been wanting to say for a while, Clair.' My heart spasms. 'When the kids came around the other day it just emphasised for me how important this is. I know you've been hesitant to let Marty and Beccy see me. I know you probably don't trust me. I know why you repaired the fence.' She wipes her nose yet again; I see the tremble in her hand. 'I understand it's hard to trust a woman who can't care for her own daughter . . .' She pauses for breath. 'Someone who's so careless she lets her only daughter die, but I promise I'll be more careful with your children than I was with my child.' She touches my hands.

'It's more important to me than I realised, but I enjoy their company. It's a pleasure for me to have them around. I'm begging you, Clair, please don't pull them away from me because of what happened to Chelsea.'

I should put my arm around her again, comfort her. I know that I should. But it is as if my head is clanging with the giant bell of my fear. It drowns out everything. I am barely even capable of hearing what she is saying. I don't want it to be like this; I want to be able to provide this woman, my friend, with the comfort she obviously needs. But I am so caught up in my own emotion, my own thoughts, that I cannot. And even as I am incapable of lifting an arm to drape over her shoulders, she looks at me quizzically, not comprehending my reserve, my inability to reach out to her. I realise this might be the end of it, of the friendship Sandy and I might have had.

There are so many things women want and need from each other: friendship; support; a reference for a new school; true sympathy when a child has been killed – but still this woman wants more. She is asking for access to my children. As if they are a gift that can possibly be shared around. Women ask so much of their friends, sometimes more than we are capable of giving. If only our needs were as simple as men's – a shared beer over the back fence, the occasional trip to a sports match together. If only.

TWENTY-SIX

*I*t is when both the kids are in the car with me, coming back from one of Marty's sporting events, that I tell them what I've decided. For Sandy has made me aware that further restrictions must be imposed.

'I'm going to talk with your father,' I say, 'but I've decided we need to do a few things a bit differently.'

'What things, Mummy?' I look into the rear-vision mirror and my eyes meet Beccy's, blue and bright, trusting.

'Changes to your routine, changes to the way you get to and from school. Things like that. We're going to be cutting back on some things.'

'Great.' I move the mirror so I can see Martin looking out the window, his chin resting against his hand.

'What's that, Martin?'

'Nothing.'

'No, tell me. I want to know what you said.'

'I said, "Great".'

'Exactly, Martin.' I nod. 'It will be great. It'll give you a chance to focus on important activities, like your schoolwork, for example.' I know I'm going out on a bit of a limb here, making major parenting decisions like this by myself without consulting Peter, but I'm pretty sure I can convince him, particularly if I use the argument that Martin's schoolwork will benefit.

'So what types of things are we going to be cutting back on, Mummy?' Beccy is leaning forward slightly, all the better to hear what I have to say.

'For one thing, Martin's playing too much sport.'

'Mum! I am not.' Suddenly Martin's hand is down from his face, his eyes glaring at me. 'You and Dad like me to play sport. That's what you've always told me.'

'We do, Martin, but at the moment you're playing too much. It's affecting your marks.'

'But Mum, I always get okay marks!'

'Exactly. Think how much better you could do if you didn't spend so much time playing sport. So you'll have to pick just one sport and stick to it.'

'One! That's ridiculous, Mum! How can I pick just one?'

'You can and you will, Martin.'

'What about me, Mummy?'

'You'll be the same, Beccy, limited to one activity. You must choose between gymnastics and dancing and two sessions a week at most.' This is hard, what I'm doing. Beccy loves both those things, and is very good at them; she's just been picked for the representative gymnastics team and is in the dancing performance group.

'Oh, Mummy!' Beccy sounds as if she will cry.

'And from now on I'll be taking you to school. And picking you up.'

'No bus!' Marty is incredulous, and angry. He leans towards me. 'How will I see my friends now? I'm hardly allowed to go anywhere anymore.' He throws himself back against the seat.

'Well, Marty, you know your friends are always welcome at our house. I've told you that.'

'As if they'd want to. It's not like we're allowed to do anything.' It is muttered under his breath, but still I hear it. This time, however, I don't ask him to repeat what he's said.

'There's one other thing.' I can't stop now, even though for me this is the hardest part of what I need to tell them, the crux of it really. 'You are never, never, to go back into Chelsea's yard without me knowing, do you understand?'

From Marty there is stony silence, from Beccy a little nod. 'Okay, Mummy.' The softness of Beccy's voice is almost enough to break me. I've always wanted to give my children everything that their hearts could possibly desire. To spoil them, lavish treats upon them, let them feel like a prince and princess, but that is not the way to be a good mother. None of this is easy. I remember an email that was once sent to me: *I'm a mean mother and I'm proud of it.* That's the type of mother I am now, the type of mother I have to be – the mother who looks after her children properly, even if it means that at times they might dislike me.

TWENTY-SEVEN

*M*ornings are the worst for me. The great gulf of the day stretching before me. Anything can happen over a day. Anything can happen over a minute. A child can die. A child can decide they won't take any more and put the rest of their life in danger. I rise in the morning and know these thoughts will play in my head over and over. My fear looping within my brain, weighing on everything I do, settling into a feeling of dread about what may come.

I force myself to exercise, hard. Sometimes this helps, the electric current of my fear dropping for a time, and I sleep a little better. But I don't walk past Sandy's house anymore, and I no longer go outside when Mel is hanging out her washing.

I have bursts of frenetic activity now, scouring the house from top to bottom. For when I do sleep, I dream – horrible dreams that wake me in terror. In my dreams the police come. It's the red and blue lights shining through the window, onto the ceiling of the lounge room, that gives them away. They come quietly, but they can't hide this, their flashing lights. I know they will come into my house and uncover the secrets I want so desperately to hide.

There are so many ways a person can reveal themselves – a word, a gesture, the shedding of skin. I cannot cocoon myself properly, cannot hide myself and my children from the world and its prying eyes, and I am terrified that everything has the potential to give us away. Once I'd believed myself and my family safe in this suburban enclave, broken fences and all, because I knew what lay directly behind those fences and felt comfortable with it. It was always the world beyond that worried me – and now it is everywhere, those who would harm my children are everywhere, even pressing against my house. I and my children are safe nowhere.

I wipe down every surface in my house with the strongest bleach; I wash my children's sheets and clothes so that nothing remains on them, so they can tell no story of where they have been, who they have seen, what they have done. By erasing everything around them, making it new and clean again, I will eradicate the past, make possible a new future, make my children safe, so that I and they can begin again.

Both Mel and Sandy ring from time to time, inviting me over, suggesting outings, but always I refuse. Being with them would not help; it would only make things worse. And I don't let my children play with Tabby and Sam as much as they used to.

I resign from the Parents and Friends Committee and quit my job. I can't focus on the minutiae of petty school and work concerns when there are more important things for me to do now, things at home that require my constant vigilance.

In the long, long period of time between when I drive my children to school and when I pick them up there is far too much opportunity to think, and to worry. Scenarios run in my head, over and over – broken bodies, ruined lives – a looping newsreel impossible to stop. I watch the children now, more closely than ever. I listen to what they say to each other and to anyone else they talk to. When you are a child, the truth can slip out far too easily. Whenever Marty gets a phone call from a school friend, I can't help myself; I pick up the other handset so carefully that I'm sure he can't have heard. But his conversation is always stilted and he doesn't stay on the phone long, so I wonder if he knows what I am doing.

I know that Peter is increasingly concerned about my behaviour. But I can't tell him what the real trouble is. He is the children's father after all, not their mother; he wouldn't understand in the same way I do. I also mistrust his reliance on authority; I cannot be sure that he wouldn't go to the police with any truth I tell him. Even with him, I'm concerned about what the children might say. And so I trail Peter and the kids when they attempt to go off together. The mother who is always there. They don't quite tell me that they would prefer not having me around all the time, but almost.

Years ago, before I had children, a friend told me about an acquaintance of hers who had degenerated into a state of almost constant paranoia after her children were born. They couldn't walk on the outer edge of the footpath for her fear of them being hit by a car; they couldn't stay alone in the house without their mother for even a minute at a time; she had to know where they were every moment of the day. In my pre-children days that story made me laugh. It seemed so absurd. I'd read about the adaptability of children: babies falling from third-storey windows and surviving, orphans growing up to have full and productive lives. Children were robust, I'd believed, resilient, capable of surviving many things. What I didn't realise at the time was that these were children in the abstract, children who existed in some time and place separate from me, children I hadn't nurtured with my own body. Children who didn't mean the world to me; children for whom I wouldn't do anything, anything at all.

TWENTY-EIGHT

I wake from a sleep that has not been enough, never enough these days, no matter how many hours I spend in my bed, eyes closed, body not moving. No matter how much sleep I have, it is no antidote to the wakeful hours of clenched watchfulness, protecting, shielding my children from dangers so numerous, from corners so undefined that it almost stops my heart to even consider them.

It's a Saturday morning, Peter not home, again. If he was a different kind of man I would suspect an affair, but I know he's like me – too concerned with duty, too concerned with providing for his family, too busy, too tired, to consider something which, in the end, would simply be too much trouble. So with my husband safe at work, it's not the possibility of an indiscretion that worries me. It takes me some time to realise what's nagging away at the back of my mind. It's the silence.

Early Saturday mornings are television time in our house. The children, not allowed morning TV on school days, make up for it on the weekend. By now the television should be on, the kitchen a riot of used bowls, dropped cereal, spilt milk. Instead the television is off and cold and the kitchen is as I left it last night. I glance at the clock. 8.30. Impossible that they're still asleep at this hour.

I check anyway, pushing doors open. Beccy's room is a pink fishbowl of discarded clothes and twisted sheets and blankets. No matter how tightly I tuck in her sheets, no matter how many times I rise in the night to check that she remains covered, this is how it is by the morning – as if she has fought a battle in her sleep. Martin's room, too, is a mess, a blue mess. I haven't really realised until this morning how firmly I've sex-role stereotyped my kids. Acceptable when they were younger – perhaps – but probably it's time to repaint.

But what concerns me now is their whereabouts.

I search every room in the house, every cupboard, calling as I go. They've done this to me before, hiding quietly until I've found them, but today they will not be revealed. My rational voice tells me that of course they are all right. They're not babies anymore. Nobody could spirit both of them away without enough noise and fuss to wake me. But my imagination will not be quieted. I see the bent and broken bodies of my children, lying in a gully, disfigured by days submerged in water, abused, torn, bruised; I see them bleeding, dead and dying – a montage of emotion, battering, overwhelming. It is only when I stand on my back deck, peering into the garden looking for them, and see movement in the house behind that I realise where they are. And that reality is almost worse than the darkest of my imaginings.

I dress myself so quickly that my pyjama top is thrown behind my bed and it will be weeks before I find it again, dusty and festering with the emotions of that morning. It is my exercise clothes I pull on now, dull with the smell and patina of yesterday's sweat.

I half-walk, half-run to the corner, right and right again. It is less than three minutes from realisation to now, me standing in front of this door. Sandy opens it.

'Are they here?' I try so hard to keep the anxiety from my voice, but I wonder, can she see the images and the terror behind my words – the broken bodies, careless words, my children's innocence which could serve to destroy them?

But Sandy is laughing, the sun bright on her hair, and I remember the first day I saw Chelsea and it is almost more than I can bear. 'Oh Clair, I'm so sorry, did they worry you? I was going to wait a little longer and then ring you, but I didn't want to wake you.'

'So are they here?' It's almost a snarl, relief and anger and fear tripping over each other as one emotion asserts itself and then the next, before they settle together into an emotional morass very close to hopelessness. No matter what I've done and told them, my children do this to me, slipping away when my back is turned, while I am sleeping, waiting for the moment that I'm disarmed. We're told to keep our children safe, look out for them, but no-one ever tells us how hard this will be.

Without waiting for an invitation I push through the door. Sandy follows. They are in the kitchen, my children. As on that first day I visited Sandy, the sun is streaming through the windows. The benchtops, their black covers removed, glitter in the brightness. It is like entering another world, one where a vestige of hope has returned, and I realise that, for all her sorrow, Sandy has been granted a strange kind of freedom. The worst that could happen to a mother has happened to her, and she has survived. It is behind her; nothing like that will ever threaten her again.

Is this life's true freedom? The drinking from the well of true despair, the knowledge you've reached the nadir of your life, can trudge no lower and that you've survived? Is that the only way you can remove the shackles of your daily fear, by being completely gutted to a point of emotional emptiness? If that is the case, then religion has a lot to learn. Forget years of prayer, deprivation and self-sacrifice in the attempt to remove oneself from earthly desires and attachments. Probably Abraham had it right when he was poised to kill his only son, before the voice of God stepped in and denied him the true sorrow which contains the only real possibility of rebirth. Sacrifice your first-born, face the most horrible reality that you are capable of conceiving, and in comparison everything else for the rest of your life will be easy.

Is this why people do things so horrible they are almost beyond comprehension? Drown their own children, kill their parents, their partners? Is it because without such abhorrent, extreme acts they are incapable of facing the fears and demands of everyday life? Is it only by comparison with something more horrible than the life we normally lead that we can be truly free?

My children look up at me, seemingly guileless, but I see the shift in Marty's expression; my children's presence here is not an accident. Marty has come here deliberately, in defiance of my wishes. It is here in this house, not mine, that the cereal is spilt – a chocolate cereal that I do not allow my children to eat – the milk bottle opened and not put away. My children are so comfortable here, so at home, that I can't help but wonder if this is the first time they've visited like this. And what does this mean for Sandy, this relaxed abandon of my children? Does it remind her of Saturdays when Chelsea still lived? Or is this perhaps a different type of reality, a new way of existing where her child does not live but others do, and there is some company and comfort to be had from that.

I would like to believe either situation holds, but the reality is more complicated. This is Sandy's deliberate doing. This woman has invited my children here, like a witch to her sugared house so she can capture their very essence: their warmth, their joy, the easy way they fit into their skin. She is alone, desperate, not content with the memories of what she once had, determined to take what is not hers. And my children have made it easy for her, following their noses and their stomachs. With a deliberate disregard of what I have told them, they have walked into this woman's trap. She will suck them dry with her need and her questioning, reduce them to shells, so they will be forced to tell her the truth of what happened *that day*. And then, only then, will she be satisfied because my life, and that of my children, will be as ruined as hers.

I stand between Beccy and Marty, facing Sandy, trying to keep control of my voice. 'I'm very glad that the children are here, but really, I have to insist this doesn't happen again. I woke up and they were gone – no noise, no note. You can't imagine what I thought, how I felt.'

Sandy is nodding, and I realise I've chosen the wrong line of attack. Here is someone who *can* imagine. I start again, 'It's not right that they impose on you like this.'

'It's not an imposition, Clair. Your children have never been an imposition for me. Not when Chelsea was alive and not now.' She looks at them. 'If you've finished you can watch the TV in the lounge if you like, so your mum and I can talk.'

She's right, the children shouldn't be here while we're talking like this. But it's not Sandy's job to dismiss them, it's mine. 'Yes, off you go kids.' But I'm too late; they've already left me.

'I don't want them coming over here like this, Sandy. How did they get here anyway?'

'Sit down Clair, please sit. Do you want a cup of coffee?'

I shake my head. Without another word, she pulls out a chair and sits down. Reluctantly, I follow.

'I'm sorry,' she says. 'It could've been better done. I should have sent them home to write you a note or wake you up and let you know. It's just that I saw them in the garden and, well . . . I haven't seen them for a while, you know. And Clair, I like your children. I started talking to them and then I remembered this packet of awful chocolate cereal I'd bought the day before Chelsea died. She was always asking for it and it was going to be a surprise for her. I kept thinking I should really throw it away, but I haven't been able to. It was somehow a *relief* for me, the idea that your kids could eat it. So I invited them in. I met them at the end of your street; it was all completely safe.'

It is so simple, the way she says it. A cereal bought for her daughter, never eaten, unable to be thrown away. So simple, no premeditation, no guile, no ulterior motive. So simple and so untrue.

'And then you talked,' I say.

She looks a little surprised. 'Yes, we talked, of course. But I let them see Chelsea's room first.'

'You took them into Chelsea's room?' Surprise and anger – both are evident in my voice.

'They wanted to see it, Clair. And why not?' Sandy is sounding just the slightest bit angry herself. 'They miss her; they were friends. Why shouldn't they spend a bit of time in her room? You didn't let them speak at the funeral. You don't like me talking to them. I can see they don't have friends over much anymore. In fact they told me that. They have grief as well.

That has to be acknowledged. They have to have some way of expressing it.'

'I give them ways of expressing it. All the time. I'm always there for them; they can talk to me any time they like. Did you know that Peter got a counsellor in for them?'

Sandy shakes her head.

'No, I'm sure you didn't know that. But we have to be allowed to deal with their grief, as their parents, in the way we think is best. And you popping up like this and inviting my children over and taking them into Chelsea's bedroom, as if it's some kind of shrine, and feeding them the cereal intended for her is not helping me and it's not helping them.'

Sandy speaks softly and slowly. 'Is it possible, Clair, that you might need to talk to someone yourself? Perhaps Chelsea's death has affected you more than you realise.'

I stand up so quickly that my chair rocks and almost tips over. 'I'm sorry about Chelsea's death. And yes, it *has* affected me. But now I'm ready to move on. I'm ready for the children to move on and this type of thing is not good for them. My children are never to come over here without me again. Do you understand that? If it happens again I'll call the police. I'll make sure Martin and Rebecca are aware of that as well.'

I sail into the lounge room and taking the kids by the hand, I exit the house. There is no doubt that my friendship with Sandy is well and truly over.

Beccy is crying; Marty is sullen – his habitual mood these days. 'That is not to happen again. DO. YOU. UNDERSTAND. ME? You have disobeyed and ignored everything I've told you. You are not to go over to that house without me ever again. And in fact we will probably never go again as a family. I'm very, very angry with Sandy. She shouldn't have invited you in. She shouldn't have shown you Chelsea's room.'

Marty has his arms crossed, refusing to show emotion, but suddenly Beccy is gulping with sobs. 'Why not, Mummy? Nothing bad happened. Sandy was nice to us. She always is. And I asked if I could see Chelsea's room. I was starting to forget what it looks like. And you know what, Mummy?' She looks up at me. 'It still smells a little bit like her. Just a little bit.'

Now I am crying too. I realise it's the first time I've cried since Chelsea died. Great salty tears are draining my body of substance. I huddle on the floor in a ball. It is too much for me. Everything that I'm expected to bear. I don't know how much longer I can go on like this. I look up at both my children. 'You have to be careful, that's all. Don't you realise that if anyone finds out what you did the day Chelsea died you'll be taken away from me? I might never see you again.'

Beccy comes over to where I am still huddled on the floor and puts her arms around me. 'But Mummy, all we did was because of what Chelsea did first. You know that, don't you?'

I begin to rock as I answer her. 'I know that, darling. I know that all too well.'

TWENTY-NINE

I've seen how the other children look at mine in the playground. They cast their sidelong glances; I see them talk behind raised palms, whispering to each other, whispering about my children.

Marty comes towards me while I wait in the car, his head down, his backpack pulling and bumping against one side of his body as if he can't be bothered to put it on properly. He doesn't say goodbye to anyone as he leaves, his eyes sliding downwards as if to deliberately avoid contact. When I ask him how his day has been his only reply is 'Good'. There's nothing more that he will tell me. I don't hear about his school sport, I'm no longer told what he did at lunchtime with his friends. At home he takes himself off to his bedroom and does his homework without me even needing to ask him. When he's finished he sits in front of the television and watches whatever is on, his eyes almost unblinking; I'm not sure if he's taking anything in at all. He doesn't respond to the sounds of Tabitha and Sam playing in the garden next door. He no longer asks if he can go outside and play; no longer asks if he can invite other children over here.

The sport he chose to maintain was soccer. It's something he's always been good at, but his performance gradually began to suffer and one Saturday he told me he couldn't be bothered going anymore.

My children have always been a source of joy and support for me. At times when I've felt anxious or down, their very presence has been enough to lift me. So it's not easy for me to bear – this dissolution, this lassitude. I'm sorry it has to be like this. It feeds into my concern, but I know I cannot afford to remove any of the restrictions I have imposed for some time yet. Caught within the loop of my fear I can see no other way.

THIRTY

'*Your* husband tells me that you're having trouble sleeping.'

Pat is back, again at Peter's insistence, after she no doubt told him Martin and Rebecca were fine but that his wife might benefit from some one-on-one time. She's sporting the twin-set look again, this time in a different colour, accessorised with beads of a matching hue. Someone should tell her that all that matching of colour went out in the eighties. But it won't be me. Today is strictly business.

Anger bubbles up inside me and is almost welcome. A cleansing emotion, which if used properly can cauterise some of the rotting gunk created by my worry.

'I never sleep well. Peter doesn't usually notice. Perhaps the fact he's noticing now means he's the one sleeping worse than usual.'

'Perhaps.' Pat nods her head, beads are set a-clinking. 'But today we're here to talk about you, about how *you're* feeling. So you don't feel you're sleeping worse than usual?'

I shrug. 'No better, no worse.'

'Would you like to talk about Chelsea's death? How it's affected you?'

'Chelsea was one of my children's closest friends. I knew her well. Not only do I have my own sorrow to deal with, but also the sorrow of my children. I recognise this. I'm dealing with it. It's not always easy, but one can't expect something like this to be easy.'

'How are you doing that – dealing with Chelsea's death and helping your children to deal with it?'

'I'm keeping them busy. I'm making sure that they have lots of time to spend with other friends, in supervised situations of course. I'm making sure they spend time on their homework. I don't want this to distract them, to throw them off course too much. As far as I can, I'm trying to make sure their lives continue as they were before this happened.'

Pat leans back a little in her seat. 'But of course they can't be exactly the same, because Chelsea isn't around to play with them anymore.'

I'm beginning to feel annoyed. What does this woman expect me to say! 'Look Pat,' I respond, 'Chelsea lived behind us for a little under six months. Yes, Marty and Beccy were good friends with her, but there was a life before her and there'll be a life after her.'

'That seems like a very practical way of approaching things.'

'I'm a very practical person.'

'But perhaps your children aren't, and can't be expected to be, as practical as you.'

'Perhaps not, but as their mother it's my job to guide them, my job to help them cope with what's happened. I'm doing that as well as I can.'

Pat tilts her head to one side. 'We've talked about your children a lot, and obviously you're working hard to shield them from what happened, but I suppose even that must be having some consequences for you?'

'Not more than usual.' I lean forward, feeling distinctly irritated now. 'Look Pat, do you have any children?'

'One, a girl who's nearly eighteen.'

'So you know. You know what it feels like to have a child.' Now that I have begun I cannot stop, the words fall from my mouth. 'You know that you're always worrying about them: when they cry because they're teething; when they take their first steps; the first time you leave them with someone else; their first day at school; the first time you suspect they might have been left out, not invited to a party, or bullied; their first day at high school. You tell me, Pat, what comes after that? Their first date; the first time they do drugs, drink alcohol, have sex. And then? Their first job; the first time they move in with someone, get married, have a child. Are they attractive enough, smart enough, resilient enough, do they have enough money, enough common sense? *Everything, everything, everything.* How do we ever let them walk out the door? How the fuck do we ever do that?'

I've revealed far more of myself than I intended and I slump back in my seat.

'You worry about these things a lot?'

'Just all the time, Pat. All the fucking time. And don't you see, in the context of all the other things I worry about as a mother, Chelsea's death is just one more thing. Sad, tragic, but, you know, just one more thing.'

'One more thing that impacts on your life and your children.'

'If you want to put it like that, yes.' I raise my palms upwards, give a slight shrug. 'You know, I'm sorry about Chelsea. I truly am. But she's dead now and I've got my two kids to worry about. They're my priority, as they always have been. As they always will be.'

'I sensed this, Clair, very much when I spoke with the children. Martin says he feels he's been cut off from his friends. No outside visits. Friends can only come here; he can't go anywhere else. He feels he must hide from you, Clair, if he wants to keep in contact with his friends.'

'I've explained to you,' My voice is cold; there will be no more discussion, 'I'm being the best mother I can. There's no way anyone can criticise me for that.'

My heart is beating faster than it should. Pat's words have done it. *He feels he must hide from you, Clair, if he wants to keep in contact with his friends.* Those words made me think. What exactly was Pat talking about; how could Marty keep in contact with his friends without me knowing? And then I realise.

What I'm doing is justified, I know that. But it's so different from what I experienced as a child. I could have left my open diary in front of my mother and she would have closed it and returned it to my room. Was it out of respect for my privacy, or a profound sense of indifference? I don't know her reasons, but I have never had any qualms about digging into my children's private world. It is another way to keep them safe. The world in which I grew up was a simpler one; at least behind the closed doors of your home you were safe – strangers couldn't enter without you even being aware of it. Now almost every house has a gate perpetually open, the greatest broken fence of all – the internet. I'm sure this is what Pat meant when she said that Marty must hide from me to contact his friends – the internet.

Marty has had an email address for a long time, several in fact. I'd helped him to create his first during his mid-primary years. It'd seemed like a great idea at the beginning, a way of introducing my son to the wider world, but it hadn't stopped. He'd created more as the whim took him and then there were forums, chat rooms, instant messenger,

more and more ways for him to have access to the
world through gateways which could not be easily
closed. Many of these were now sanctioned by the
school via class home pages and school chat rooms.
I'd argued against them many times through the
Parents and Friends committee, argued the point that
such systems simply made it easier for bullying and
inappropriate behaviour; they provided a way for
children to be accessed even when they'd not chosen
to give out their address details to other children,
but each time I'd been overruled.

Over the years, Marty has settled on one main
email address and I check that from time to time,
more so lately. I'm careful, clicking onto only those
messages that have already been opened; I've no
desire for Marty to know what I'm doing.

I should have realised that his usual account has
been little used lately. See how easily things slip your
notice if you are not very, very careful?

I click onto the 'history' icon on his computer
screen and there it is, an email account I've never
seen before. I don't even have to guess the password
– Martin has checked the box that keeps him permanently signed in.

There aren't many messages and I see that the latest is from Tabitha, already opened. I click on it, my hand shaking slightly.

Marty I've been thinking. It'd be easier if we told the truth. Maybe we're doing the wrong thing. Maybe we should tell someone what really happened. I'm sure they'd understand.

I hadn't realised the danger was so close.

'I've cancelled our broadband.'

Marty's watching TV; it takes some time for his eyes to properly focus on me. 'Are we going back to dial-up? You know that'll be a lot slower, Mum. You mightn't be able to use eBay.'

I sit down beside him. 'Yeah, I know, but that's not what I meant. I mean that I'm cancelling our internet subscription completely.'

'Why?'

'Because the internet is dangerous. There are too many stories of children being stalked online, and cyber-bullying. I've decided that cancelling the internet altogether is the best thing to do.'

'But Mum! You've taken away my mobile. I can't visit friends anymore. The internet's the only way to keep in touch with a lot of friends. If you take that away then I'll have nothing! I need it for schoolwork anyway. What did Dad say about this?'

'I'll discuss it with him when he comes home tonight, but I haven't finished yet, Martin. You're not to visit Tabby and Sammy without me knowing. In fact, you're not to talk to them at all. They can come over here, but you're not to go over there. Is that clear?'

'Perfectly.' He turns away from me, not bothering to argue, not even bothering to put up a fight. But I don't know if that's because he really intends to obey me, or if he's already planning another way around me.

We bump into Mel and her children at the supermarket. She acts as if she's both surprised and happy to see me, reaching over to give me a spontaneous hug, patting my shoulder and then pulling back to look me in the eye. 'Clair sweetie, I can't believe I need to come to the supermarket to see you. How are you? I haven't seen you in so long.' I feel myself shrinking from her; the good humour and zest, which once seemed so attractive, grate on everything – my ears, my eyes, my mind.

I force myself to talk with her: *How are the children? Good. How's work? Good. Peter? Joe? Good. Good.* It's the type of conversation you have with just a fraction of your brain engaged, for as I talk to Mel, it's the children I'm listening to and watching – Tabitha in particular. She has on a big green crystal ring and it catches the supermarket lights, throwing emerald flashes against Martin's white shirt. Beccy is hugging her around the waist. My daughter's eyes are red-rimmed as if she's been crying; the truth is she often looks like that now. I see all four children lean in together, whispering urgently – so much to say, so little time. I see Tabitha take Marty's hand and pull him towards her. I hear her say in a voice just loud enough for me to hear, 'Maybe it *would* be the best thing for us to do, Marty. Tell people what really happened.' I hear Martin reply, 'You promised, Tab.' And that's when I wonder exactly how far I'm prepared to go in order to help my children.

THIRTY-ONE

That night, Peter and I have the worst fight we've ever had. He holds himself back until the children are in bed and then he comes into the lounge room where I'm giving the floor another clean.

He turns the vacuum cleaner off at the wall and then stands in front of me, arms crossed. With a sigh, I put the nozzle of the cleaner down and sit on the couch. I knew it would come to this soon enough.

'What the hell's going on, Clair?' Peter asks. 'Marty tells me that now you're cutting off the internet to our house. You've stopped work, quit the P & F, taken away Marty's mobile phone, Marty plays hardly any sport, Beccy doesn't do gymnastics anymore.' He ticks everything off on his fingers. 'I've been supporting you on all this, hoping that this, this . . .' He runs his fingers back through his hair. 'Oh God, I don't even know what it is. I just hoped this over-protectiveness of our kids would somehow wind down or something. But it's getting worse, Clair.'

I give a slight snorty laugh. 'Let me get this right. You're concerned because I'm protecting our kids? I mean, I could understand if I was abusing them, but I'm not, I'm looking after them.'

'You're not looking after them, Clair. You're restricting them. Kids need some room to move, to grow.' He drops his shoulders. 'It's like you're cutting off their circulation.'

'They're fine, Peter. This is how kids need to be looked after. We should've always been looking after them like this.'

Peter raises his hands to his forehead and then drops them in frustration. 'You can't be serious.' He shakes his head. 'What you're doing is excessive, Clair. You need to see someone, and I mean someone more than Pat.'

'What is it you're suggesting Peter?' I ask coldly.

'You need to see a doctor. Someone who can give you something to help you get over this . . . this obsession.'

'Oh right, I see. You want me to go and see some anonymous doctor in some anonymous surgery and tell them the details of our family's lives so I can get some drugs to knock me out.'

'You don't have to see an "anonymous" doctor Clair.' He uses little finger quotes around 'anonymous'. 'Why don't you go and see our regular doctor?'

'Like that'd be any better.'

I don't want to admit to Peter that I've already considered his suggestion. But I know I wouldn't be able to do it. Our regular doctor knows me as the person I once was: someone who managed; who had healthy, well-nourished, well-dressed children with the usual childhood complaints, nothing more. How could I admit to her now that everything I once managed so beautifully is crumbling around me? How could I bear to have her judge me? She is an efficient doctor, skilful; she shepherds patients in and out, their problems solved with a legible script and a few words. How could I sit before her and explain what's happening to me when I wouldn't be able to tell her why? How could I stand to be there as she surreptitiously looked at her watch and thought of her next patient, her lunch-break, what she's having for dinner? It would be unbearable to go before her as I now am. But I'm not going to admit that to Peter.

The truth is that I want to open up to Peter, to tell him the extent of what I'm feeling: the fact that it's almost impossible for me to get up from my bed when there's no-one at home; how, in contrast, I can't sleep at night and I wander the house like a grey ghost, tidying, folding clothes, sometimes even making meals to freeze for some future, as yet unseen, eventuality; how, if I return to bed, I feel as if my heart is rising in my chest and choking me; the fact that I feel like a racing car on choke, permanently revving, the adrenaline coursing through my body. The sense of dread that pervades everything I do. If only I could tell him all this. But I can't tell Peter any of this because he would want to know why and that I won't reveal; it would be the worst betrayal of the children possible.

'Anyway, Clair, whether you're willing to go to a doctor or not, I've also decided some things,' says Peter. 'I'm giving Marty my old mobile phone, we're not having the internet cut off and if Beccy wants to do gymnastics again then she's damn well allowed to!' And with that, he storms out of the room.

'I'm their mother,' I scream at his back. 'I'm the one who knows what's best for them!'

I don't care if Peter thinks I'm furious with him. Better that than have him glimpse the true depth of my despair.

I don't sleep at all that night, and the next morning, when everyone has left, I return to bed, my room darkened, a pillow pressed against my throbbing eyes. I breathe deeply in and out, attempting to calm my renegade body. The fight with Peter has upset me more than I'd realised.

That is when I hear it, the acoustics performing their trick again.

It is the soft sigh of Sandy's voice. 'What a beautiful day. Too beautiful to be inside.'

And Mel's laughter. 'A bit cool for me. But I guess I can manage it for a while. For you, sweetie.'

They seem to be sharing a coffee on Mel's back deck.

'It's just so nice to see the sun,' Sandy continues. 'Autumn's not even finished, and already I'm looking forward to spring. Dreading it too. Chelsea always loved spring. The smell of jasmine and the promise of buying new clothes!' Sandy laughs now. 'You know how much she liked new clothes.'

'I know.' There's a rustle; perhaps Mel has placed an arm round Sandy's shoulders. 'Her and Tabby both. They would've been forever sharing clothes as teenagers.'

'Wouldn't they just?' There's sadness in Sandy's voice, but a kind of wistfulness and a hint of pride as well. 'They would've been the best-dressed girls in the neighbourhood.'

'Oh Sandy, they *were* the best-dressed girls in the neighbourhood. You know that!'

'They were, weren't they? And little Beccy. Now she has a sense of style, that girl. What a wonderful little character!'

'She looked up to Chelsea, didn't she? Even after such a short time she loved her like a sister. I think she loved her as much as she loves Tabitha and that's saying something!'

Sandy is crying now, I hear the quiver of her voice, the rough breathing coming through her words. 'Oh Mel, thank you for this. Thank you for understanding that I need to talk about these things. I need to know that other people loved her, that other people do love her. You can't know how much that means to me.'

'I know, darl. I do know. I'm here, Sandy. I'll talk with you as much as you need me to.'

There's silence and then Sandy speaks again. 'Is Clair home, do you know? I haven't seen her in days.'

'She's around. I see her bringing the kids to and from school. But I don't see her much at other times.'

'The house seems closed up. She keeps all the blinds at the back down now. I never see her hanging the washing out anymore. Did you know we had a fight?'

'No. What about?' There's the sound of sugar being stirred into a cup, a sound filled with so much simple domesticity, the promise of an uncomplicated life that could be lived without fear. But that is not for me. I know that now.

'The kids came over to visit me a few weekends ago. I saw them, you know, outside. I so rarely see them anymore. They told me Clair was still in bed and they hadn't had breakfast yet so I invited them over and they stayed to have something to eat. It was so nice, Mel. And then Clair came over and she was so angry at me and Marty and Beccy. I felt sorry for them.'

'Those kids are so good,' says Mel.

'I know,' replies Sandy. 'They've got more sense than Clair at the moment! Anyway, she dragged them home that day. I honestly don't know what's wrong with her, Mel. I'm worried about her, but I'm worried about Marty and Beccy more. Maybe Clair thinks something's going to happen to the kids if they spend time with me. She must think that because I couldn't even look after my own child, I can't be trusted to take care of anyone else's.' She begins to cry again.

'Oh, darling, you can't blame yourself for this, for how Clair's reacting to Chelsea's death. We know it wasn't your fault. It wasn't anyone's fault. We all know that. Clair's always been a bit like that. You know, just a little bit of a control freak.' She laughs gently to reassure the other woman and I can imagine her holding her fingers slightly apart to illustrate the extent of my controlling tendencies. 'It's just that before this happened she was able to manage things.'

There's the sound of Sandy blowing her nose. 'I sensed that about her when I first met her, you know.

I thought I could help her. That's why I made such efforts with her. I thought I could help and now look at what me being here has caused.'

'I've tried for years. When things are going her way she's all right. The moment things swing a bit, she's off. I've learned to kind of ignore her during times like that. You know, I nod and say any old rubbishy thing, like *that's wonderful, oh do you think so?* Half the time I don't think she even listens to what I'm saying!' There's the sound of Sandy's laughter. 'Eventually she kind of burns herself out and things settle down again. I feel a bit sorry for Peter, though. I don't know how he lives with her sometimes.'

'Well I'm glad it's not just me! But she was very angry when Marty and Beccy came over. When she left, she told me she'd call the police if they ever came to visit me again.'

Mel gasps. 'That's terrible! I have to admit she's never said anything like that to me. What did you do?'

Sandy gives a half-snort. 'Well she kind of stalked off before I could do or say anything.'

'She oscillates, you know. Sometimes it's as if she can't get enough of you; at other times she doesn't want anything to do with you. Somehow you're expected to be attuned to that without her telling you.'

'But I am just worried for the kids. I never see them outside anymore. Marty's at an age when he should be having friends round all the time.'

'I know. Tabby and Sam really miss them. They grew up together, you know. They're almost like brothers and sisters. But that's always been part of Clair's problem. She never thinks of the effect her actions have on other people.'

'How have your kids handled all this? Has this affected them terribly as well?' Sandy's voice is in danger of cracking again.

'Oh sweetie, please don't blame yourself for anything. You're the one who's borne the greatest tragedy of all. My kids are all right. They'll never forget Chelsea, they loved her, but they'll move beyond it.'

'So they're okay?'

'Yeah, they're okay.' She pauses, 'Well, Tabitha's got something on her mind; I can see that. We're going away the weekend after next. She's always a lot easier to talk to when we're away from home. I'll take her for a long walk on the beach, have a chat with her, see what's worrying her. But I'm sure she'll be okay. I don't want you to fret about her, or Sammy.'

So that is the truth of what they think of me – just as there can be no pretence in someone's behaviour when they're unaware they're being observed, nor can there be any pretence in someone's words when they're unaware they're being listened to. But it's not their opinion of me that's of concern; no, now I have something concrete to worry about – what Tabitha might be about to tell her mother.

It's midnight. There's a frightening clarity at this time of night, achieved when a mind's only obligation should be sleep. I am wide awake and considering my options. They are so few and time presses, presses.

I have decided there's only one thing left for me to do. I think about how Sandy attracted my children to her home with something as simple as forbidden chocolate cereal; I consider the story of Hansel and Gretel, the witch luring the children to her house with the promise of food more plentiful and more delicious than anything they had tasted before. And I wonder, what exactly would be sufficient enticement to lure Tabitha into my gingerbread house, alone and unprotected?

THIRTY-TWO

*I*n the end it's not that difficult. The truth is that all children are vulnerable. Not just me as a child, not just my children or Chelsea, even strong-spirited Tabitha has her weak spots.

It was simply a matter of using a computer at the library to send an email from Marty's email address to Tabitha, explaining that he had a friend at school – 'Julia Ray' – who'd met Tabitha briefly after netball some time ago and wanted to know if Tabitha would like to meet up on a particular chat site devoted to girls and fashion. According to the email, the more friends 'Julia' could convince to come onto this site, the better her popularity rating would be. So Marty had offered to pass on Julia's email address to Tabitha.

Did Tabitha want to join Julia on the chat site? You bet she did. She emailed back almost immediately to Julia's newly created address. So easy to construct a personality within a virtual land where no-one checks that you're really who you say you are.

Amazingly, Tabitha found she had many things in common with this sophisticated older girl – music, clothes, sport. They began trading emails, several times a day, and then I laid the bait. Would Tab meet Julia after school? They could get to know each other better, Julia suggested, be best friends, share all their secrets. Tabitha was excited by this suggestion; she had a big secret, she told Julia. Something she was dying to tell someone. That was all I needed to know to confirm my fears; Tabitha wasn't going to be able to keep things to herself much longer. So I moved quickly – within only a few days, the two girls agreed to meet each other at the mall after school.

This last part was a bit harder. I knew – even if the fictitious Julia didn't – that Tabitha wasn't allowed to go to the mall after school. I knew arrangements would have to be made without Mel knowing. Luckily Julia was flexible enough to agree to meet Tabitha at a time which would allow her to leave school a little earlier, meet up with Julia and still be home at the normal time. Mel wouldn't even know where Tabitha had been. So easy; too easy.

I watch Tabitha sitting at a table in the food court, patiently waiting for Julia to arrive. I know, of course, that there is no Julia to come, there is only me – watching, waiting; only me wondering if I can really go through with what I have planned. For this is true madness; I am well aware of that. It is as if I am about to step off the edge of the world, nothing beneath my feet. I know that after this there will always be a divide to my life – the time before and the time after the terrible act I am about to commit. I have managed to get to this point only by keeping my mind occupied with the careful planning required in order to ensure Tabitha keeps her secret. Details of what is necessary garnered from crime dramas and from my own dark imaginings. How quickly it has come to this. Only a few short months ago I was an ordinary wife and mother; now I teeter on the edge of the abyss, true horror at its bottom.

And yet I have no choice. That is what I tell myself. My children's futures depend on me being strong and succeeding; this time I am fighting for them. There are many steps that have led to this and there's no escape from the path I'm now on. I can't back out. My fists are clenched tight, I feel my fingernails pressing hard against my palms.

I remain patient. Tabitha has bought a drink and she is almost finished. I know this girl so well, almost as well as my own daughter; I see that she is trying to look sophisticated, unconcerned, but still it is obvious that she is becoming increasingly restless, looking at her watch, glancing around her. That is when I move over to her.

'Hi Tabitha,' I say, a friendly lilt to my voice. I've practised this for some time at home, the lightness of it, the slightly questioning tone as if I'm surprised to see her. 'What're you doing here?'

Tabitha looks up at me, a guilty shadow flitting across her face. I don't usually see her in school uniform, and without the colour she normally wears she looks pale, washed out, a little sick, vulnerable. She is still so young, the soft lines of childhood not yet gone. 'Oh hi, how're you.' She frowns. 'Aren't you going to be late picking up Marty and Beccy?'

'They're having an afternoon with their dad,' I reply. I pull out a chair and sit down next to her. 'I was doing a bit of shopping. What about you?'

'Umm, well I'm supposed to meet a friend here.' Tabitha looks behind me, to the left and the right. 'But it looks like she's not coming. I didn't have much time anyway and I've got to go now. Mum'll expect me home soon.' She reaches over to pick up her school bag.

'No worries,' I say. 'I'm on my way home now. I'll take you.'

Tabitha is unable to look me in the eye. 'Mum'll be expecting me to come home on the bus. She'll kind of wonder why I came home with you if I do.'

I laugh. 'Oh I see. That's how it is, is it? Your mum doesn't know where you are.' I lower my voice. 'What about if I drop you at the corner, and you can walk home from there? Your mum won't know and I won't tell her.'

Slowly Tabitha nods. I can see that she's uncomfortable, but she's been caught out and she knows it. 'Promise you won't tell Mum? I've never done this before and I wouldn't want her to worry.' Tabitha's forehead is wrinkled with concern.

'I promise. I won't tell anyone I saw you here. No-one will ever know we met up. I promise you that.'

I have to keep swallowing to force down the bile that is rising in my throat. I haven't been able to eat all day and there is nothing in my stomach apart from that vile green liquid. I'm terrified of what is to come next, but I've thought things out so carefully. Everything has gone according to plan so far and there is no reason for me to fail, nothing to stop me now from doing what I need to do in order to silence this girl. This is what I continue to tell myself as we, Tabitha and I, walk through the shopping mall towards my car.

I have my hand in the small of Tabitha's back. We're nearly through the exit doors closest to where I have parked the car. We are nearly there, so close.

Then I hear my name being called.

I turn, and see the last person I could have imagined; the last person I could have wished for. It is Mel coming down the escalators towards us. She has both hands above her head and she is waving.

I feel my breathing become more shallow. I have an almost overpowering urge to rush through the doors, taking Tabitha with me; to throw her into the car, lock the doors, speed away and pretend that Mel has never seen us and we have never seen her. But it's too late. My children's future is shattered.

Mel takes the last steps in one bound. Turning to Tabby, she says, 'Tabby, darling, what're you doing here? Why aren't you on the school bus? I was just about to go home so I'd be there when you got back. What are you doing here anyway?'

Tabitha's head is lowered; she cannot look her mother in the eye. I know how reluctant she will be to tell the truth. 'I came to meet a friend.'

'Who?' Mel looks at me for a moment, including me in her confusion.

'Umm, well, kind of a friend I made online.'

'Online! Tabitha! I've told you you're never to meet up with someone you've met on the internet.'

'But this is okay. Julia's a friend of Marty's. She remembers me from netball. Marty gave me her email address. She's allowed to come to the mall after school so I said I'd meet her here.' Tabitha tips her chin up defiantly.

'What's this Julia's last name?'

'Ray.'

Mel looks at me again, drawing me into the circle. 'Do you know this Julia Ray, Clair? Is she one of Marty's classmates?'

'I'm not sure,' I reply slowly, trying to buy time to think. 'I might have heard the name.'

'I'll have to ask Marty about her.' Mel's brow is furrowed. 'I don't like this Tab sweetie. I don't like it one little bit.' She turns to me. 'Were you going to give Tabby a lift, Clair?'

I nod and try to smile, the effort isn't successful. There's a lump in my throat, an obstruction to my breathing. 'Yes,' I manage to say. 'I saw Tabitha sitting by herself and when I found out what she was doing here I thought it'd be safest to take her home.'

'Thanks for that, Clair. Sorry you had to get involved in this.' She gives Tabitha a gentle whack on the bottom. 'Come on madam. Let's get home. You and I have got some things to talk about!'

THIRTY-THREE

For years I believed I'd successfully escaped my past. I thought I'd left it all behind me – the anxieties and misery of my schooldays.

The problem, I now realise, is that it's all still there. Even as a successful adult, with a loving husband, with two children who are attractive and clever and good at sport and have friends – all of these things are not enough. The scars of bullying do not show merely on my knees, they are embedded in my psyche. Chelsea's death has ripped off the old scabs and what is beneath is raw, blistering skin. I'm nothing more than my fears and my insecurities, unable to escape my past, unable to imagine a future with hope.

And if this has been the legacy of my childhood, then how can my children be expected to survive what *they* have been through and what is to come when Tabitha reveals the secret she has been keeping? Particularly when there's a strong chance that my children will inherit my own dark imaginings. Once I'd believed that keeping my children safe within the confines of their own home would be enough, but now I have learned that even within your home there are dangers. The truth is that I can't do this anymore.

I tried to save Martin and Beccy from the consequences of what they did to Chelsea – pushed as they were by my words to them – but in the end, my actions since then have only made things worse. I've failed to protect my children. Just as I failed to protect myself against Sharon all those years ago.

I didn't sleep at all last night thinking about this. Now I've reached as far as I can go. I know that a life not lived is better than a life that feels as mine does: anxiety, fear, depression, self-loathing, dread – all the time. I've done as much as I can, there's only one thing left. Now I will defend my children from this world in the only way remaining.

I am crying as I make my final preparations: affix the hose to the car; run it through the back door of the garage, under the shrubs and into my bedroom; tape the gap in the window; pull the curtain. The last moments of tears. When the children come home I will be bright and cheerful. It will be a good meal, a warm bath, a cuddle in bed. I will tell them that tomorrow life will go back to what it was: they will be allowed to visit friends, play whatever sport they want; tomorrow they will be free and they will believe that everything will be all right. And then I will save them.

Despite the rift that exists between me and Peter, I'm sorry for what he will find, but there's nothing I can do about that either.

THIRTY-FOUR

*I*t is the rainbow girl, the slip of a girl – Tabitha – who stands at my door. In my bedroom, at the back of my house, I'd almost decided not to answer the insistent knocking, but in the end, the habits of a lifetime are too strong for me to do anything as rude as that. I realise now that I'd heard Mel's car pull out just a moment ago. So Tabitha's been home from school today and has seized this moment of unsupervised freedom to visit me. Now she gives herself to me like this, now that I have no will or energy to do anything about it.

I take her into the kitchen. She sits at the table dressed in orange and white. I've never seen her look so serious, like an ancient sage capable of unravelling the strands and secrets of a lifetime. I'm not afraid of her; by now I'm beyond all fear – I'm heavy and tired and resigned to what must come next. There's nothing this girl can say or do that will make anything worse.

I offer her juice, a glass of milk, a biscuit; she shakes her head. 'No, I don't want anything. There's something I've got to tell you . . . before I get too scared. I realised yesterday this is the only way to stop what's going on . . . how you're hurting Marty and Beccy . . . and Sam and me too. I don't care anymore if Marty says we shouldn't. Some secrets aren't worth keeping. Even if you think you're protecting someone. This secret's been too dangerous. I need to tell you.'

I nod, but don't speak. I have no desire to stop her.

'Chelsea was always threatening things, you know. But we never really believed her. It's a bit like Beccy always threatening to come inside and get you if we don't do what she wants, but usually she doesn't, usually we manage to sort things out okay. With Chelsea, if we didn't do what she wanted, she'd always say something like, "I'm going to make you all feel sorry for me one day, and then you'll feel bad and it'll serve you right." She said it so often that we got used to it and we never really believed her, but on the day that she died, she was really angry.' Tabitha raises her head to look at me, her face is drawn. I nod again, encouraging her to continue, inhaling quietly as she does so.

'That day, we were teasing Marty about a girl at school who liked him. We all knew that Chelsea didn't like us talking about other girls liking Marty, so we were teasing her a bit too. Chanting something like "Jade loves Marty, Marty loves Jade". Chelsea was cross with him, with all of us. She told Marty that if he didn't say he liked her better than Jade she was going to go really high on the swing and then jump off and hurt herself and then he'd be sorry. Marty laughed; he knew what Chelsea was like – he didn't believe her, none of us did. But then she got on the swing and *did* begin to swing really high. Suddenly we were all scared. Chelsea was actually doing something for a change, not just talking about it. We all started yelling and trying to get her to slow down. Beccy and Marty even tried to stop the swing from going so high so she wouldn't hurt herself, but then it happened. Chelsea *fell off*. She lay so still and then we could tell what'd happened and that's when Marty decided what we were going to do next.'

'We can't tell anyone what happened.' Marty pulls his eyes from Chelsea's still body, looks at the other children, scanning them, urging them to listen to him. He's already calmed the screaming of Beccy and Tabitha and the two girls are sobbing now, Beccy beside him, Tabitha on the other side of the circle. Sam's face is white and drawn. Marty knows that it will be a matter of moments before an adult is with them. His whisper is sharp and urgent. 'She did this because she wanted to make us all sorry for not being nicer to her. She did this because she was angry with me for not admitting I liked her better than Jade. As if she didn't know that! She didn't mean to do what she did. She just wanted us to feel sorry for her and pay more notice of how she was feeling, but not this.'

The other children nod. They know. How many times have they wanted sympathy and attention – from their parents, from their friends? How many times have they contemplated something like this? Thinking about throwing themselves down the stairs in order to scare Mum and Dad, pretend to have a cough, all so they can get warm hugs and attention. They've all thought about it. What none of them has ever had is the determination to carry it off like Chelsea.

'We tried to get her to slow down; we told her to. I know she was silly for not listening to us. I know she shouldn't have done it. But she wouldn't want anyone to know what she did. It was stupid; she didn't mean to kill herself and you know her mum and dad'll be really upset if they find out. We mustn't ever tell what happened, do you agree? We have to look after Chelsea. It's what she would have wanted us to do. We have to agree this was just an accident. DO YOU AGREE? Tell me!' Quick, urgent. 'Tell me we're never going to tell anyone what she did.' He shakes Beccy, looks directly at Tabby and Sam. One by one the children nod, unaware of just how much that promise will cost them.

And me – just how much has that promise cost me?

I am crying great rivers of tears – dark and black, they are leaching everything from me. It is not only the good that is going, not only the bad, it is the beliefs of a lifetime. I am crying away my fear, my tension, my past.

How can it happen like this? So suddenly, as if the world has been tipped upside-down and nothing will ever be viewed in the same way again. I see now, there is more than one way to look at things; there is always more than one way. I had seen something the day Chelsea died, had seen certain actions and my mind had constructed a story around them, a story that reflected *my* past, *my* life, *my* experience, a story that had no basis in fact.

I remember how I crawled beneath the broken fence the day of Chelsea's death. How in that moment of transition, in that liminal space – freed from the constraints of one side or another, one reality or another – I had, for a moment, been able to look at the world from another perspective, that of my children. I had seen a world without limits, without barriers, and in that moment things had seemed clear and bright and uncluttered: the ground so close to my face that every blade of grass was seen in stark relief; the cold feel of water through my jeans; the smell of the sun on the bark of the tree – sensations uncloaked from the artificial covering of the emotions, expectations and disappointments of a lifetime. How had I not understood then? How had I failed to grasp the gift that had been given to me for a moment – the ability to view the world with completely fresh eyes, freed from the shackles of my past?

But now this orange-clad slip of a girl has given me a second chance and I wonder – is it too late for me; is it too late for any of us?

EPILOGUE

We're not camping, *that* would be a little too much, but the three cabins are arranged around the fire pit which is where we'll sit tonight, roasting our marshmallows and remembering.

The sound of laughter drifts from Sandy's cabin. She and Mel are in there with Beccy and Tabby. I think they're braiding hair, or experimenting with make-up. Sandy and Mel will each have a glass of wine in hand; the girls will be giggling and preening. I imagine the movement of the women together, the casual touch of hands and bodies, the mingling of warm breath. The intimacy of these things, the shared moments to which I'm not privy, no longer worry me; I'm happy to sit here and listen to the laughter, to relax and think, to be alone.

Beccy spends a lot of time with Sandy now. The fences around my house are no longer broken, but neither are they 'fences' in the true sense of the word – a barrier, a means of defence, something built to contain my life and exclude others. I've had gates built between our house and Sandy's and Mel's; they stand almost perpetually, deliberately, open.

We have responsibilities as parents, as mothers, but there's no reason they can't be shared, fears discussed, children learning from more than one or two adults who love them. And, of course, we also have responsibilities towards those we choose to be our friends.

Sometimes Beccy sleeps over, in Chelsea's pink and white room. I don't know if Sandy ever intends to change that room, but there's nothing wrong with that. It gives Beccy comfort, and, while we've not directly discussed it, I'm sure that it comforts Sandy too. Tonight Beccy may sleep in Sandy's cabin, or with Tabitha, or with us. It doesn't matter and the decision is hers.

I see the men – Peter and David and Joe and Sammy – coming back through the trees. A couple of hours ago they took their shiny new rods and tackle boxes, and childhood memories of fishing, and set off with a strong desire to show the women just what good fishermen they really are.

No matter what Peter has returned with – a fish or ten, a stretch of seaweed – I will allow him to explain to me the fight it put up. He will decide how to cook the fish tonight and when. Some of these things – the letting go of responsibility for so much – still do not come naturally to me. The habits of a lifetime do not change quickly or even completely – but I'm learning. In a few weeks Peter and I will do the once unthinkable: we'll have a week away together, without the children. It will be good for us, will cement what we are gradually moving towards. My husband no longer works as hard as he used to; he spends more time at home, more time with me and the kids. I've put on some much-needed weight – fattened up, as he laughingly tells me – and there is a growing abandon in my body which both of us recognise and encourage.

And what of Marty, possibly the one I hurt most of all?

He's been on a three-day soccer camp. He'll be dropped off here tonight by the father of one of his friends. He's playing soccer again, will play cricket in season and swims three days a week. He no longer bites his fingernails and has a new email address, the password of which I don't know, even though I still often discuss with him the need for good internet security – not all responsibilities should be forgone!

I no longer watch my children play – well, I do occasionally – but it's more an act of nostalgia than anything else. I know the danger of that watching now, the possibility of making assumptions about a misheard word, a misunderstood action, of believing that things can be understood in one way only. And I also know that sometimes we need to trust our children to handle things on their own.

None of this has been quick and easy, none of it has been without a struggle – one doesn't come back from the edge of madness in a hurry. In fact perhaps one never completely comes back from somewhere like that – but I'm willing to accept help from others now, and I know that life is only ever a series of tiny, frightening inching-forwards moments. One day at a time, one step at a time. Day by day I push through the fear and doubt; sometimes it is easier than others, but it is never entirely without effort.

In the days following Tabitha's visit I took the most difficult step of all – the first. Flowers in hand, I made my way to Sandy's house. I knew there was no real way I could apologise for my behaviour, but I did tell her how sorry I was for what I'd said. On that day, I told her how Marty had felt about her daughter, her Chelsea. I held Sandy's hand and explained that Chelsea was the first girl Marty had ever loved, that he would have done anything for her, that she would forever hold that most special of places in his heart. Sandy cried and I let her, holding her against me, knowing that these tears were necessary. And when she had quietened, I asked Sandy if it would be possible for me to have a copy of the most recent photo of her daughter she possessed.

For the next step was to acknowledge Marty: his feelings; his maturity. By the time he returned from school that afternoon, Chelsea's photo was framed and sitting on his bedside table. He never said anything directly, never thanked me, but that night, for the first time in many weeks, he gave me an unprompted kiss before heading to bed.

When next I spoke to Mel, I told her about the troublesome window; she merely thanked me, but a few weeks later they had a screen erected. Now voices from their back deck are deflected away from my bedroom. It is easier for me to sleep. I should have been more honest with her years ago. Thankfully, she didn't follow up too far on the 'Julia Ray' emails. Perhaps she thought it was one of Marty's friends playing a joke on Tab, and she simply treated the incident as a reminder of the need for good internet security.

Slowly, I've shared with both Mel and Sandy some of the issues I still struggle with. Mel admits her sister has similar problems and Sandy has lent me a number of books on anxiety and depression. I know the two women are true friends, always there for a chat or a cry if I need it. Everything helps.

Despite my continuing struggles, there are many things that bring me joy now and one of them is to see Tabitha dressed in orange. If I'm shopping and find something in that colour and in her size, I often buy it for her. She is a beautiful girl, a soul wise beyond her years, as are my son and my daughter – as perhaps are all children when they're given half a chance.

Today is the anniversary of Chelsea's death. That is why we're here. It's not a celebration, but it is an acknowledgement – of her life, of the sorrow she left in the wake of her death. We will remember her, we will cry, and we will support each other.

I know now that life is not living *without* fear, life is living *despite* fear. It is being uncertain, terrified, and still waking day after day, still having the courage to put one foot in front of the other and carry on. Time and love, support and understanding, perseverance and determination – they are probably the things that have the greatest chance of healing human lives. I know they are the only things that have helped me to heal mine.

ACKNOWLEDGEMENTS

*E*ven though I try for it not to be the case, writing a book involves sacrifices from those who love you. As always, it is those closest to me who have to put up with the most – my husband, Mladen, and children, Luka and Tiana, have stayed close to me on the roller-coaster ride of a journey that writing *Broken Fences* proved to be. They gave me time when I needed it and support when at times the writing seemed terribly emotionally close to home.

In the case of *Broken Fences* the influence of my family was also more literal. Mladen was the one who almost forced me to write down the dream which I had while we were on holiday and that became the entire story of *Broken Fences*. Luka and Tiana, and their relationships with their friends, strongly influenced the characters of the children. I have always believed that children have far more common sense than most adults give them credit for and that is certainly the case with my two!

I need also to thank my parents and extended family who are always hugely excited about whatever is next in store and whose support is both emotional and practical. As well, a huge bouquet for all my friends who have always shared their conversations and stories with me. I hope that *Broken Fences* brings forth a lot more of that!

While strictly speaking this is not a 'Varuna' book I still want to mention Varuna The Writer's House and all the people who support it because without Varuna I might never have been published at all. I believe Varuna and its Creative Director, Peter Bishop, play a hugely important part in fostering and encouraging Australian literature.

Thank you to Pippa Masson from Curtis Brown, my agent, who has ably steered me thus far through the often scary white-water of contracts, foreign agents and, even more foreign, foreign contracts.

Again the Hachette Team have been wonderful: Vanessa Radnidge, who is much more than a publisher to me and who is never afraid to make brave publishing decisions. Amanda O'Connell who did a fantastic job of editing all the way through, from raw material to printed novel. And finally Sandy Weir and her team who always know exactly how to turn my words on paper into something that the rest of the world wants to pick up and read.

BROKEN FENCES
CAMILLA NOLI

Introduction to *Broken Fences*

'Now is not the time for letting go.' (p 165)

When Sandy, her husband Dave and their daughter Chelsea move into the house that backs on to hers, Clair insists that she and her children Beccy and Marty 'officially' welcome them, although she's aware that the children have already met and become enamoured of their pretty and outgoing new neighbour. On the surface of things, as Sandy and Dave settle in, they get on well with Clair and her husband Peter, as do her other neighbours Mel and Joe, and their kids Tabitha and Sammy. But it almost immediately becomes clear that Clair feels her safe and comfortable life is threatened by the arrival of these new neighbours, despite their seeming affability. She fears the influence their forceful and charming child has on her children and becomes increasingly protective. Her reaction to the 'danger' represented by the new swing (p 28) built for Chelsea is the first inkling of her deep-seated insecurity regarding her children. The novel builds on this fear, gradually revealing her neurotic insecurity, and some of the events in her childhood that have led to it. When the children become disgruntled by her restrictions, about which Chelsea criticises her to them, Clair construes the criticism as jealousy of her care for them as opposed to Sandy's casualness (p 107), revealing just how neurotic she's becoming. A shock accident, though, propels her further into a dangerously psychotic state of over-zealous protection of the children whom she believes are at risk. But perhaps Clair, herself, is the real danger to her children, not the imagined fears outside their home?

Cleverly beginning with a shocking prologue, this novel keeps its readers in a state of escalating suspense. Noli weaves a web of psychological tension which tightens and stretches until the final chapters in which all is revealed. On one level this novel is concerned with the tenuous boundaries that exist in a community between friendship and enmity. Central to it, though, is the exploration of the conflicting emotions felt by any mother, torn between a desire to protect her children and the realisation that from birth, her children are moving steadily towards a release from her control.

About the Author

Camilla Noli lives on the Central Coast of NSW with her husband and children. She is a graduate of the Varuna Writing Program in Sydney's Blue Mountains and *Still Waters* was her first novel. *Broken Fences* is her second. http://www.camillanoli.com/

Reading Group Questions for *Broken Fences*

Broken Fences is a chilling account of how maternal love can go seriously awry unless checked by reason and restraint. When fuelled by bad experiences in her own childhood, the love of a mother can in fact sometimes become quite deadly. Camilla Noli has provoked many questions in this novel, which, although it deals with an extreme case, has much to challenge anyone who has ever been a mother, or the subject of a mother's love.

1. *'I'm a mean mother and I'm proud of it.'* (p 198) Motherhood is obviously a source of real interest to Camilla Noli, whose first novel, *Still Waters*,

also dealt with maternal feelings – in that case, the lack of them, and in this case an excess of them. Compare the two mothers in these novels.

2. The question of what mothering should consist of is constantly explored in this novel. eg 'We won't be very good mothers if we keep second-guessing everything we do.' (p 76) OR 'That's the whole trick, isn't it?' I replied. 'Let them feel adventurous when really they're completely safe. It's the whole trick of mothering really.' (p 32) OR 'We need to keep them safe from the outside world, not welcome it in.' (p 169) How should a mother balance her desire to protect, with a desire to teach children self-reliance?

3. Recent events in the media bear a startling resemblance to the one predicted in the prologue of this novel; families rent by depression or conflict are often destroyed by those closest to them. Did this novel help you to understand the origins of such crises? Discuss.

4. The novel raises the question of childish innocence and need for protection, and the child's

capacity for both ill intentions and responsible adult decision-making. Clair ponders on the fact that: 'All children are like quicksilver, unable to be stopped, ... treacherous' (p 8) and on the 'rules and whims of children – informal, ad hoc, uncontrollable.' (p 12) Chelsea is the embodiment of that wilfulness, whereas Tabitha proves to be the embodiment of a wisdom beyond her years. Discuss the capacities of children for both adult failures and strengths.

5. The suburban enclave presented here, with men at work all day, and families 'safe' at home (p 20) may be typical of some areas but is by no means universal. Sandy corrects Clair when she calls their way of life 'normal': 'the life we have here is special, absolutely not normal ... If we truly think that we can control everything then we're in for a big shock one day; we're setting ourselves up for it.' (pp 74–5) Is Clair's malaise a western middle class one? Is affluence partly to blame for her obsessive behaviour?

6. The novel raises the question of how, despite the fact that women since the 1960s have been

raised to believe that they can choose a career, many still opt not only for marriage but for full-time parenting. Clair says that 'it was my children who breathed a soul into my existence' (p 19) and later explains to Sandy that: 'What I hadn't bargained for, what I hadn't even been able to imagine until it happened, was that I would love my children with a love so powerful that it made everything else redundant.' (p 73) Clair's reliance on her children is shared by many women who devote themselves to their offspring, to the exclusion of almost everything else. Is this a healthy way to live?

7. The novel suggests that Clair's neurosis has been fuelled by the slights suffered in her childhood, to which she refers on a number of occasions eg 'far better than I'd been protected' (p 76) OR 'than I'd ever been prepared by my own mother'(p 109) OR 'I've experienced the loss of a friend, so I know how my children feel.' (p 127) Peter comments on the way Clair used to wear her hair which is explained chapters later when she frees her hair in order to hide from a barrage of torment from her ex-friend Sharon

and her group (p 130). She reflects that 'things had happened to me that made it difficult for me to completely trust other people enough to let them too far into my life' (pp 54–5) and is reminded of her childhood by Beccy's grief: 'old hurts and rejections are not forgotten ... you will never be free of them.' (pp 39–40) Does Clair make too much of Sharon's rejection? Or does bullying always leave such a deep scar on the recipient?

8. Clair believes that barriers are necessary to protect us from others. 'At least *they* were contained by decorum and social niceties, by the fences that were supposed to delineate spaces of individual responsibility and obligation ... that were meant to act as a barrier and not be ignored.' (p 29) Her first reaction to the accident is to have the fence between theirs and Sandy and Dave's house mended so that her children can't crawl under it anymore. Robert Frost once wrote a poem entitled 'Mending Wall' which includes the line: 'Good fences make good neighbours.' You can read the whole text at: Famous Poetry Online <www.poetry-online.org/frost_mending_wall.htm>

Discuss the poem in relation to this novel. Do we need such divisions to maintain our independence, or are they used to bolster our insecurities?

9. Clair refers at one point to: 'Just one of the many performances that make up all our lives.' (p 30) and later that: 'to have said no to Sandy that day would have marked me out . . . as a different person to the one I'd presented myself as for years.' (p 63) Do we all play 'parts' in our lives?

10. The novel presents two sides of the question of whether neighbourhoods are friendly or threatening places. On one hand Clair writes that: 'Friends are the cement of a community' (p 45) but when she reveals her insecurity about Sandy becoming part of Marty's school community and possibly threatening her position as a prominent member of the P & F, she reveals the fragility of such neighbourly bonds (p 62). Are communities potentially supportive, or hotbeds of intrigue, in your opinion?

11. Clair is honest with herself when she confesses to her 'Fear that my control over Marty and Beccy

is eroding faster that I'd realised.' (p 192) when she also fears that Sandy is 'asking for access to my children.' (p 193) There are few people in our lives over whom we have such licensed control, as we do over our children. Do we use parental concern as a way of assuming power in our lives, and is it perhaps a manifestation of insecurity as well?

12. Internet access (p 223) proves the lie that children can ever be protected from the outside world. Discuss.

13. One of the things full-time parents must learn to deal with is what is referred to as the 'endless afternoon' of parenting (p 58). Is the boredom and repetition of the routine of daily family life one of the things that has pushed Clair over the edge? Can you sympathise with this?

14. Clair refers to 'this first step towards welcoming people into your life so that they can hurt you properly.' (p 139) Is this a pessimistic view of relationships, or simply a realistic one? Are all relationships destined to end in some form of

hurt? And if the latter, is that necessarily a bad thing? Discuss.

15. Noli cleverly changes Clair's first person account from past to present tense (p 110). Why do you think she does that?

16. 'Through our actions, through our lack of action, we decide our future; we can make ourselves vulnerable or strong, victim or aggressor. And sometimes we have no other choice in life, no other responsibility, other than to act in order to protect ourselves' (p 133). Discuss the implications of this statement.

17. Clair's reaction to the accident is to think immediately: 'perhaps I can save my children from the enormity of what they've done' (p 114) and later of: 'how best to protect my children from the consequences of their actions.' (p 118). Her immediate concentration on the feelings of her children and her determination that she can protect them is chilling, in that she also seems not to feel anything for a dead child or the parents. Later when she realises her mistaken

interpretation of the accident, we as readers might interpret that as her inability to see her children as anything but victims in need of her care. Her refusal to allow them to create their own eulogy is another evidence of this. Discuss.

18. 'I know now that life is not living *without* fear, life is living *despite* fear.' (p 264). Discuss.